Welcome
Church
Library

Very proud to be a Black Country working class lad, Colin was born in 1948 in Wednesbury in the West Midlands, the seventh child of Stephen and Frances Nicholls. He was educated at Joseph Edward Cox Primary School and Charlemont Secondary Modern School. In 2005 he gained an Honours Degree in English Language and Literature at the University of Central England in Birmingham. In 2006 his first book of poetry was published entitled, *In My Mind's Eye,* and in 2007 Pegasus Elliot Mackenzie published his first novel, *The Turn of The Worm*. His second collection of poetry, *Star Gazey Boy,* was published in June 2008. He is now thrilled to have this opportunity to introduce his second work of fiction, **'*Scrooby*' The Pilgrim Fathers.**

The reviews Colin received for his first work of fiction delighted him because as he explains, 'It is always satisfying to have your work acknowledged by others'. He therefore is even more concerned that his second novel should live up to that of his first. It is of a completely different nature, using names taken from the official passenger list of the *Mayflower* and based upon the true emigration of our ancestors in the seventeenth century to the Americas, but it should be read as purely fictional in its characterisation and storyline.

By the same author

In My Mind's Eye
(United Press)
ISBN: 978 1 84436 157 1

The Turn Of The Worm
(Vanguard Press)
ISBN: 978 184386 355 7

Star Gazey Boy
(Vanguard Press)
ISBN: 978 184386 427 1

SCROOBY:
THE PILGRIM FATHERS

Colin J Nicholls

SCROOBY:
THE PILGRIM FATHERS

Vanguard Press

VANGUARD PAPERBACK

© Copyright 2009
Colin J Nicholls

The right of Colin J Nicholls to be identified as author of
this work has been asserted by him in accordance with the
Copyright, Designs and Patents Act 1988.

All Rights Reserved

No reproduction, copy or transmission of this publication
may be made without written permission.
No paragraph of this publication may be reproduced,
copied or transmitted save with the written permission of the
publisher, or in accordance with the provisions
of the Copyright Act 1956 (as amended).

Any person who commits any unauthorised act in relation to
this publication may be liable to criminal
prosecution and civil claims for damages.

A CIP catalogue record for this title is
available from the British Library.

ISBN 978 1 84386 470 7

Vanguard Press is an imprint of
Pegasus Elliot MacKenzie Publishers Ltd.
www.pegasuspublishers.com

First Published in 2009

Vanguard Press
Sheraton House Castle Park
Cambridge England

Printed & Bound in Great Britain

Dedication

For my sister Brenda Wilkins and her husband Gordon,
for all the help and encouragement that they
have given to me over many years.

Acknowledgements

I would like to thank again, as I did in my first novel, the diligent work of my niece and her husband, Natalie and Paul Newman, my harshest critics and most appreciated supporters, in proofreading the first copy of this work. I can always trust them to do a fine job and they never let me down.

I also give acknowledgement to the various texts and web sites that I have needed to use in research of the subject matter, in order to gain a factual background of the history of the Pilgrim Fathers, and the small village of Scrooby, Nottinghamshire, from whence they came. These I have listed in the Bibliography and I offer my sincerest thanks to all of their contributors.

Contents

PREFACE 17
CHAPTER ONE 19
CHAPTER TWO..24
CHAPTER THREE...36
CHAPTER FOUR 44
CHAPTER FIVE...52
CHAPTER SIX 60
CHAPTER SEVEN...75
CHAPTER EIGHT..91
CHAPTER NINE 116
CHAPTER TEN..146
CHAPTER ELEVEN 176
BIBLIOGRAPHY 193

Preface

Firstly my sincerest apologies goes out to those who were kind enough to purchase my first novel, *The Turn of The Worm,* and having hopefully enjoyed that have on its strength purchased *Scrooby*. I had no idea whatsoever how or what I might write about but I really wanted not to be a 'one book wonder'. So why the Pilgrim Fathers? Who knows? The mind works in strange ways; doesn't it? The apologies of course are for the entirely different direction in which my mind has taken me. Does anyone want to read a novel about the Pilgrim Fathers? Is the history too distant for us all to give a damn? When anyone asks me about my poetry they inevitably ask, 'Well why did you choose to write about this or that particular topic?' I have no definitive answer to that question but I do know that in most instances I did not choose a particular subject, it chose me.

I do know though that the easiest and quickest poems that I have written always happened to me rather than me choosing for them to happen. Whereas, the most difficult ones that I have written have actually been about those subjects that I have set out to write about.

'SCROOBY' The Pilgrim Fathers could not be further detached from the previous novel. Is the subject interesting? Well, yes I believe it is. The amount of work I needed to put into *Scrooby* was fourfold that of the previous novel. It is simply a work of fiction, a historical adventure but based very stringently upon the true facts. The research I have carried out in order to complete it, I hope, makes it all worthwhile. I certainly know a lot more about the subject than I knew previously, and I do hope that if nothing else, those who choose to read it will become more historically aware of those events that led up to this fascinating emigration of our ancestors in the early 17th Century.

Chapter One

Royalty and Religion

Following the death of Jesus Christ upon the cross, and the resurrection thereafter, emerged the followers of Christ, 'Christians'. For 1500 years Christian worship was embodied within the Catholic Church. Evolution within religion created discerning worshippers; those who saw both good and bad practice and the need for change. Authority, however, fears change and the effects that change can bring. So, in the early 16th century, when voices were raised in protest and alternative practices preached, the protesters began to be labelled as 'Protestants', simply being a derivation of the word protest. Across Europe there was a desire for change to practices within the Church. Leaders emerged in Martin Luther and then John Calvin, who championed different ideas of how God should be worshipped to those accepted within the Catholic faith. Such alternative approaches towards faith, whilst enhancing the opportunities of choice, also led to a lack of harmony and unfortunately for those with zealous natures, disagreement, hatred and death.

King Henry VIII's disagreements with Rome and their Catholic principles in the 16th century highlighted the question of religious choice. Should England be Protestant or Roman Catholic? Could not the various parties of religious persuasion cohabitate in harmony? In 1521, Pope Leo X had honoured Henry with the title of 'Defender of the Faith', because of his prior support for the Roman Catholic Church. Within 13 years, however, Henry had broken with Rome and made himself head of the Church of England. This followed the dispute and controversy surrounding his divorce with Catherine of Aragon and led to his excommunication and initiated centuries of religious conflict within the British Isles. When Henry died in 1547 there had still been no resolution to the religious question and in the short reign of Edward VI they still remained unanswered. Queen Mary, who was of the Catholic faith, followed Edward after his death, and against his own wishes, having named his protestant cousin Lady Jane Grey as his heir. Following the previous years of decline of Catholic superiority, she began to restore both its authority and power. During the last three years of her reign, three hundred leading Protestants were burned alive, earning her the ungodly name of, 'Bloody Mary'. Burnt bodies and rolling heads preceded Elizabeth I, and in her long reign, she should have had ample time to resolve some of these issues. She too made small progress and instead of resolution there was a continuation of opposition and disharmony.

In 1570, the long threatened excommunication of Queen Elizabeth I was pronounced by Rome. Again this placed English Catholics in a very invidious position. Publicly most remained loyal to the Crown but privately they must have been disheartened and in disarray. The 'Papal Bull' had this to say of Elizabeth:

1. 'this woman, having seized the crown and monstrously usurped the place of supreme head of the Church of England, together with the chief authority and jurisdiction belonging to it, has once again reduced

this same Kingdom, which had already been restored
to the Catholic faith and to good fruits, to a miserable ruin.'

It continued comparatively with regard to Henry, Mary and Elizabeth:

2. 'Prohibiting with a strong hand the use of the true religion, which after its earlier overthrow by Henry VIII (a deserter there from) Mary, the lawful Queen of famous memory, had with the help of the See restored, she has followed and embraced the errors of the heretics.
She has removed the royal council, composed of the
nobility of England, and has filled it with obscure men,
being heretics; oppressed the followers of the
Catholic faith; instituted false preachers and ministers of impiety…and that impious rites and institutions after the name of Calvin, entertained and observed by herself, be also observed by her subjects…'

Hardly recognisable to us as the 'Good Queen Bess' that British history admires for her ready wit, stirring eloquence, exploration of the New World and strength of leadership. After all, she had authorised the victorious battle won against the Spanish Armada and brought to an end the constant conflicts with France.

Henry, Edward, Mary, Elizabeth who next to follow; Defender of the Faith or Persecutor of Choice? At which end of the Royal religious seesaw would the next grim-reaper choose to sit? Every time the throne received a new occupant England changed faiths and the inevitable persecution followed. The English commoner, generally illiterate, most being unable to read would have to tread extremely carefully in their choice of religion and their intensity of belief. The Protestant faith had inaugurated a shift in religion and the educated and discerning had by now begun to splinter into separatist organisations. A growing consternation developed with regard to their radical views that sometimes led to their persecution. The most notorious of these during the 1580s being cited as the, 'Family of Love', of whom John Rogers' text of that time was both anatomised and demonised. Every occurring death of a Monarch inevitably must have brought some fear within all religious circles for their future risk and fate.

* * *

James, the Protestant son of Mary Queen of Scots, (who became to be known as the wisest fool in Christendom) and was also James VI of Scotland, introduced harsh anti-Catholic laws when he came to power, but none was ever sufficient to satisfy the lust of the Puritans. Religious unrest was a black cloud that hung dangerously above the heads of the nation. The people suffered greatly because of their divided religious beliefs. All religious services had to be conducted in adherence to the order of 'the book of prayers'. All separatist services were banned. Any outspoken leaders were jailed. Unfounded accusations of witchcraft were being made against some, leading to those unfortunate enough being ducked in village ponds, tortured, or hanged for their beliefs. Public hysteria was whipped up amongst the poor and unlearned of society and they thirsted for action.

Those who were now at odds with their country, utterly despondent and living in fear of the cruel injustice handed out to the innocents, gradually became more organised. They moved with secrecy and began to outwit the law enforcers. Those who took great risk with their lives, in order to further support in their own beliefs, distributed leaflets. Rogue ministers secretly held religious services aware of the consequences of discovery. Eventually these small groups increased in size and were joined and supported by those with financial means. Meanwhile, religious strings still pulled hard upon Royal puppets and whoever sat upon the English throne needed to dance the piper's tune, with Catholic or Protestant persecution swinging according to the tune of the day. These were hard times for the English working class, who lived their lives according to the rules of the pompous games played by Royalty and the Parliamentarians. Times had improved since the Middle Ages; but life was far from easy and personal possessions were few. Those who considered insurrection were reminded of the fate of Guy Fawkes and his conspirators and starkly reminded of their torture and execution. So, thoughts of New Worlds and new beginnings became ever more tempting.

Chapter Two

Scrooby

The old wooden hay cart rumbled slowly up Broom ridge making its bumpy journey back towards Broombank cottage. Both the cart and 'Bella', the old liver and cream mare, had seen better days. Bella puffed and blowed, jerking hard at her harness and Stephen Hopkins teased gently at the mare's rear with the whip. Elizabeth Hopkins cried out, "Don't you go's hurting that old lady you'se great wassock, she's seen better days."

"Oh, hold ya threats Ma. I's just tickled the lass 'tis done no harm."

The tiny baby in Elizabeth's arms wailed.

"Now look what you'se gone and done, raising yer voice so!"

"I didn't raise me voice Ma. Yer can'ts blame me fer everything."

Liza tutted and rocked the baby gently to and fro with the motion of the cart, and she sighed, "Come now Constance, we'll soon be home and warm. Fret yer not."

They pulled slowly into Broombank's yard and slid to a halt outside of Stephen's little smithy shop. He immediately jumped from the cart, gently slapping Bella on her rear, and then went to assist Liza in her descent, with the baby in her arms, from the other side. It was extra difficult now for the heavily pregnant Liza who was six months into her pregnancy with their second child. She snapped at Stephen, "It's good to see you still got some manners."

"Oh holds yer tongue woman, yer knows I always helps yer down."

Stephen held Liza's arm as they crossed the muddy yard to the tiny cottage entrance. He cranked back the heavy metal handle and pushed hard upon the door. Inside all was cold and poorly lit. He said, "Light the candle gel and I'll rustle up the fire."

Liza crossed the cottage first, leaving the door still open behind. This cast a path of light to a large oak chest of drawers. She opened up the top of these drawers, sliding it out carefully, whilst still holding the baby. Inside was laid out with layers of dry sacking and Liza placed the baby gently inside. She then lifted the candleholder from the top of the chest that still held a stub of a partly melted candle. She bent down to where Stephen knelt at the hearth and she kissed him softly on his cheek.

"What's that fer, now then?"

"Oh nothing Stephen, nothing."

He tutted and stood to his feet. The kindle wood smouldered in front of him and Liza leant towards it in order to light the candle.

"I'll go and see to Bella, yer tek care."

Stephen went back through the door pulling it to behind him. He returned to Bella's side and began to remove her harness. The mare whinnied, shook her head and snorted as the weight was lifted from her. Once free of the cart he led her gently into the smithy shop and threw down some fresh hay from aloft. Then he scratched Bella lovingly behind her ear and then left, pulling the large wooden gate across behind her. He crossed to the well, dropped the pail down into the dark and then hoisted the rope till the pail reappeared, unhooked it and returned to the gate, where he leant over and splashed the contents into the old stone trough. He then returned to the well, fixed the rope, lowered the pail and again withdrew it. Then he carried the contents across to the cottage door and returned to Liza, who by now had added logs to the fire and hitched up the cooking pot.

"Yer already got water, then?"

"Just yer top it up, there ain't enough in there to quench yer thirst but I started it up anyhow."

Stephen poured a little more water into the pot and then placed the pail in the corner of the room opposite to the hearth. He then placed a piece of dry sacking across it and a broken slate to protect its contents.

Elizabeth, Stephen and Constance live in the small blacksmith's cottage in the village of Scrooby, in the north of England. Stephen and Liza both work for the local Squire at his house and land. Liza is a housemaid to the Lady, helping with housekeeping and cooking jobs. Stephen is by trade a blacksmith but with insufficient work to maintain them, in such a small village, he also works for the Squire. The villagers are a very close-knit community and religious beliefs are kept strictly to themselves. In these days it is not wise to discuss religion too openly outside of your own family. The villagers of Scrooby are concerned about the consequences of their own religious beliefs as are multitudes of others scattered about the countryside. All are frustrated with the system, see no future settlement, and live with continuing fear. Stephen moved many years previously from his family home in Abaraeron, North Wales, to look for work in these northern parts. He met Liza in 1603 and we are now in the year of 1606. Their first child Constance is just eighteen months old and Liza is presently with child six months. Their home, 'Broombank cottage', is just one of the many scattered estate cottages owned by the Squire and the only equipped smithy cottage. Their rent is peppercorn and in return Stephen must keep the Squire's horses well shod.

The fire had now taken hold and the pot was bubbling above the hearth. Liza had slowly added in whatever root vegetables were to hand and the smell was sweet. They had very few home comforts in the cottage and all slept in the same room with the fire. Constance was now awake and Liza had warmed up some goat's milk alongside the cooking pot and was gently feeding it to her. Their livestock consisted of a goat, given to them by the Squire, three chickens, given to them by the Pastor in payment for some smithy work, and a goose that Stephen had recently bought from the local farmer to fatten for Christmas. Out in the yard behind the cottage they had a small herb and vegetable plot, carefully fenced off from the livestock. This was insufficient to sustain the family but Stephen was allowed to bring small quantities of vegetables from his master's garden. There was also a very large apple tree that stood to the left of the cottage. This gave them a very high yield of large green cooking apples, too much in fact for reasonable storage, pickling, preserves and immediate use. So the remainder were used for bartering with other villagers in exchange for much needed goods. They rarely had callers after dusk had set in, and besides with their work and their religion there was little or no socialising in the village except at the Squire's home.

Liza ladled out the stew into two earthenware pots and unwrapped the sacking from around the bread. Stephen was busy with Constance, occupying himself with bouncing the little one upon his knee. She was a bonny girl and gave them little reason for concern. Because the second baby was on the way they had considered their positions carefully. However, the Squire seemed exceptionally pleased for them and so did his wife. It was due to this that they saw no reason to be afraid of losing their employment within the household. The Squire had himself been blessed with two children, both sons. It was the times in which they lived that caused graver concerns. It was fair to say that these were unstable times with great religious unrest and many divisions within society. The class system they could cope with, but the religious divisions held the greater threat. They both settled in front of the fire, upon the sheepskin, with Constance at their knees. The only warm place at this moment was at the hearth. They supped fervently at the warm stew, Liza assisting the baby as she needed to. The fire flickered across the darkened room and blended with the light of the flickering candle.

"We ain't got a bad life, have we Liza?"

"No dear, what makes yer ask that?"

"I worries about what's to become of us."

"How d'yer mean, what might become?"

"Oh don't worry yer pretty little head, I'm just being silly."

"You worries too much about everything, just enjoy yer stew and this moment, I couldn't ask fer more."

"Yeah, it's good Liza. We got a good life here with the Squire and we got our labour and things will get better, I know it."

"'Cause they will, we just gotta enjoy life, we works hard and we needs our bit of pleasure."

Stephen took Liza's empty pot from her hands, and, along with his own, he took them and placed them into the pail standing in the corner. He poured on clean water and knelt alongside the pail to wash the pots clean. Liza crossed over to the large pot above the fire, unhooked it and placed it to one side of the hearth, covering it over carefully with sacking.

"That's good fer tomorrow," she said.

Just at that moment there was a sharp rap upon the door.

"Who's that this time a day?" Liza asked.

"Well, we won't find out standing here, will we?" replied Stephen.

He crossed to the door and opened it. In the dim light outside stood the Pastor Richard Clyfton clutching a cloth wrap.

"Come in. Come in. Don't stand in the cold." The Pastor entered and as he did he removed his hat and nodded his head gently towards Liza.

"How are you both and how's that bonny lass?"

Constance was still sat upon the hearth and she smiled and lifted her hand gesturing towards the Pastor. The Pastor waved his hand to her.

"Sit yer down Pastor," Stephen said offering forward his stool. "You've walked all up that hill and at this time er night. Take the weight off yer legs."

"Yes," said the Pastor, "I'm getting all around the village, I needed to speak about Sunday. Oh! I nearly forgot these are for you," he said handing across the cloth wrap that he had.

Liza received it from him and opened it. Inside there was a dozen or so greengage.

"Thank you, Pastor, that's very kind of yer. Look Stephen." She showed them across to him and he also thanked the Pastor.

"What was that yer were saying about Sunday?" asked Stephen.

"Oh yes, Sunday. Squire Brewster says that he wants to speak to you all on Sunday."

Stephen said, "We've been down the house all day and we never saw the Squire."

"No, he'd just arrived back from his business when he called to see me. He said it was a matter of importance."

The Pastor stood up and replaced his hat.

"Anyway, I must be on my way. I have another two calls to make before I return home."

As he opened the door he added, "Thank you, I'll see you on Sunday then."

Stephen closed the door to behind him and returned to the fireside. The fire was burning very low and the light had become dismal.

"Best get to bed then Liza," he said and Liza removed Constance's little pinafore. They both removed their top clothing and all three snuggled up under the coarse hemp sheet that was strewn about the horsehair mattress that lay against the rear wall.

At 6.00 a.m. the next day Stephen was standing alongside the well, stripped to the waist, washing in the pail when Liza called to him.

"Eggs are ready, Stephen."

He replied, "I'll be in soon."

Stephen shook himself, lifted the half empty pail and threw its contents across the vegetable plot. Inside Constance was still fast asleep in bed. The fire was already lit in the hearth and four hens' eggs were simmering in the pot above it. Liza was busy warming goats' milk in another pot on the fire. Stephen walked across and kissed her softly upon the cheek.

"That smells good, Liza."

"Well, sit down now and eat it, thought yer want a coming in, yer'l have it wasted."

"What'n yer thinks this is all abouts with the Brewsters then?"

"Don't know but we'll find out soon enough, won't we?"

They were all loaded into the cart and Bella was back in harness again all before 7.00 a.m. Constance was now fully awake and laughing out loudly, she swung around her little rag doll as she sat next to her mother. Just then Gilbert Winslow rode past sitting astride his old black stallion, name of 'Satan'. He saw the Hopkins's and tapped his forehead with the cane switch that he held. Stephen tipped his hat in return.

"Was that Gilbert or John?" asked Liza.

"Gilbert m' dear, you won't see John astride Satan. That horse needs a firm touch."

Stephen pulled the cart out onto the lane and trundled it down the hillside. Bella's work was easy on the outward journey but not so easy upon the return.

"She's full on her sen today, ain't she?" remarked Stephen.

"Yeah, but she'll not be so full tonight," replied Liza.

When they arrived at the old Manor house that was the Squire's home, Stephen pulled the cart to a halt outside the stables. He jumped off and immediately went to Liza's assistance. As she walked off in the direction of the house Stephen began to unhitch the mare. He then took her inside with the others. He always did this fine weather or foul on the Squire's instructions. The Squire had seven horses, young and old; Bella had good food and company for the day. Occasionally the Squire's son, Love, would brush Bella down along with the others and give her a bit of pampering that she otherwise would not get. Liza and Constance entered through the rear, into the kitchen to find Cook, whilst Stephen left by the rear of the stables into the walled gardens.

"Bill," he shouted, "Bill."

There was no reply, so he crossed the gardens to the far side and passed through the hawthorn hedge.

"Oh there yar Bill, how be yer?"

"Fine Stephen, how be yer sen?"

Bill Latham was a younger man than Stephen by just a few years. He was a bachelor who was six feet two inches in height and broad across the shoulders and he was seldom seen without a hat. He had a thick but well trimmed moustache and even when at work in the gardens he was always perfectly presented. He was a retired soldier, a gentleman of the kindest nature. He and Stephen were more like brothers than work colleagues. Bill lived in the hayloft above the stables; he was treated as one of the family at the mansion house, fed from the kitchen and was regularly a guest in the house.

"Did the Pastor tell you about Sunday, Stephen?"

"He did that Bill; what's it all about then?"

"Well, we'll find out about that on Sunday, won't we? But I fears it's to do with more church business."

Constant bickering between the church hierarchies was leading to disagreements about church services and the church's presentation and portrayal. It was becoming increasingly more frustrating for the die-hard Puritans who wanted to operate in a fixed way but were at odds with their leaders. People were frightened to speak out, but for those with resolute and determined personalities there was a constant threat of harsh treatment. Sensibility, patience and great care were needed in the way one acted or spoke in public. The people of Scrooby were 'Puritans' and all agreed that even with Queen Elizabeth gone and the new King upon the throne religious persecution rather than improving, in fact, grew worse. It was argued by many that James, if anything, was becoming far more greatly engrossed in the church's business: working upon the new bible.

"All this will end in tears Bill, you mark my words. We're supposed all as one in God, but you see it'll all end in tears."

"I knows Stephen, the Squire had some big church callers t'other day and he's just about sick with all the harassment. He says he has to respect them and shows them hospitality but he don't agree with it all and he gets angry. He's between a rock and a hard place so he is, and he has to mind his words."

When Sunday came Pastor Clyfton led the service at the village church that was now under threat of closure. When he had finished he handed over the pulpit to Squire Brewster. Stephen, Liza and Constance sat amongst the large gathering, of which perhaps seventy or more filled the hall. Stephen looked around and nodded to all five of the Winslow brothers, Bill

Latham, Mr and Mrs Alden and young John, and young William Bradford. Bradford lived a few miles out of Scrooby but he never failed to turn up for any of the services. His home village was 'Austerfield', where their Uncle Robert was now raising both he and his sister Alice. William was self-taught and a very confident young man, not afraid to have an opinion about anything. He was also known to be very loyal and supportive to his friends. Brewster coughed to clear his throat and then began to speak in a loud deep tone.

"Some of you good folk may not be aware of the visitors I had in the week. They called themselves 'church seniors'. Well, it's fair to say that I did not like either their attitude or their advice. Now I discussed all of this with the Pastor, and he and I are as one. We either do it their way or we do it ours, and we both prefer ours. Now it goes without saying that with all this anxiety, suffering and persecution that's happening that we all need to take the greatest of care. We also need to be as one. So, if any of you feels any different then you need to speak out. We need to be true neighbours and friends. Now, as I was saying, the Pastor and I are together on this and we hopes that we speak for us all. If we don't then you needs to speak up. They all talk of reformation, but to us it's all half-cocked and they never see it through. They expect us all just to toe the line and to do it their way, like sheep but we say enough's enough. Their way is no longer God's way. You all know me and I hope you all trust me and accept that I'll stand by any of my own, so trust in my words when I say that I'll ask no man to do what I wouldn't do myself. Many of you have already spoken to us and we know your opinion, but we need those who know to help all the others to understand. We want nobody to take undue risk and we want every man to keep his own counsel. We all need to support one another and trust only those that we know. So, if any faces come poking about the village then let all the others know and watch your opinion. We have separated from the ways of the

Protestant; we believe to do things properly and to do, as God would have us do it. I suggest we all thinks about our choices. But the Pastor and I have said that's it, enough interference. You can come to the Pastor or me to discuss it, and you can talk to your own kin. The Pastor agrees that we should discuss it again next Sunday and be sure of our position. Thank you all and God bless you. Pastor."

The Pastor stepped back into the pulpit at Brewster's request and said, "Now let us all pray."

In his prayers he asked that God should guide their hands and be their steadying rock in making the right decisions.

Following the service everyone stood about in groups outside the church discussing the matter intensely. Some of the less well educated villagers were asking for advice to get a better understanding of the position. Horace and Marion Huggins walked out of the church behind their four girls and three sons. Marion caught hold of Liza's arm and stopped her to ask how she and Stephen felt about it all. Marion was a respected member of the Scrooby community, always available for anyone in need and she never failed to attend any village birth, or, if needed, the laying out of the dead. At the church gates two men of very contrasting heights, Miles Standish and Joseph Longfellow, stood talking. Longfellow, contrary to his name, was only five feet six in height, whereas Miles Standish was at least six feet two. As Stephen reached the gate he stopped to speak with them.

"It's hard times boys, hard times."

"Yes, but I believe we're doing the right thing," replied Miles.

Longfellow added a word of caution.

"These are very dangerous times we're a living in. We need to be extremely careful, be on our guard at all times, and not trust anyone outside of our church."

Edward Spenser joined the group, coming to Stephen's side and greeting them.

"Where's the missus Edward?" asked Stephen.

"Oh she's talking to Marion and Liza, they're making a fuss of young Constance, no doubt. She's very fussy with children us not having been blessed with our own. She's a good woman though my 'faerie Queen'."

Miles nodded to Edward and agreed, "It's a bad job you having no little babbies yer sen, Edward. She is a good woman, tis true."

Longfellow asked for Edward's opinion of their present predicament and the amount of risk that they were all taking. He knew that Edward was well travelled and was knowledgeable of the present state of affairs. Edward agreed that it was a dangerous affair and told them that in other villages men had been taken away never to return after they had been caught out practising illegal religious rites. But he agreed with them all that a man should follow his heart and that where God was concerned there was no wrong.

Chapter Three

Three Months On

Stephen tended to the bubbling hot pot of water that hung above the fire whilst Marion knelt across Liza's writhing body. Outside, in the smithy, Mary and Janet Huggins played with Constance in the straw whilst the Pastor John Smythe stood talking to Horace at the well. From inside they could hear the screams of the tortured mother who had now been in labour for over two hours. They listened intensely until the sound of a screaming child's voice suddenly filled the air. Shortly after this Stephen appeared in the doorway of the cottage. He shouted with immense pride, "It's another girl, thank God, it's another girl!"

Both of the other men rushed to his side to offer their congratulations and to enquire about the mother's condition. They were reassured that she was doing fine. Just then Marion appeared alongside Stephen in the doorway, wiped her brow with her turned up pinafore, and pushed passed Stephen turning only to mutter, "Go to yer wife, she needs yer now."

Stephen returned inside to find the new baby snuggled close to her mother's breast. He knelt beside them and stroked Liza's hair. Bending slowly he kissed the little girl upon her cheek.

"Who's this little un, then?" he asked.

Liza replied, "Meet Damaris."

Stephen studied the little Damaris, hesitated, and then asked of his wife, "How are you?"

"Better now I's seen her," was her reply.

"She's a little beauty, ain't she, Damaris yer say?"

"Yes, I thought so, after me old Gran, 'Damaris Adey'."

"Damaris it be then," Stephen said, acknowledging his wife's request.

Liza, forever the most thoughtful of hosts in whatever the circumstance, suddenly reminded Stephen, "Don't yer be forgetting our guests. Offer them a drink."

"I will do woman, just give us a second to count me blessings, won't you?"

"You'll have time enough fer that. Fetch Constance to see her sister."

Stephen returned to the doorway and shouted to Constance across the yard. She immediately came running. Stephen took her hand in his, told her she had a new sister, and led her across the room to her mother's side. Liza said, "Now go do what I tells yer."

Stephen immediately left to see to their guests.

Later that evening, having been left a sufficient period for recovery and admiration, the Hopkins's received another visitor. The door rapped and Stephen opened it to find the Squire beaming down at him. He was bearing gifts, he clutched at two pig's trotters wrapped in damp sackcloth.

"Here have these, to strengthen the missus up, so my wife says."

In his other hand he held an earthenware jug. He raised it to Stephen and said, "This'll do to toast the child."

It contained some of his strongest apple juice and Stephen quickly obliged the Squire by snatching up two clay pots to pour the liquid into. Raising the pot above his head in a fine gesture he declared, "You have to wet the babbie's head and say your thanks, God bless you all and good health."

The Squire stayed for a short while and departed, in his words, 'not wishing to tire the mother further'. He suggested that Stephen 'Take two days break from his duties but to be bright and early upon the third'.

Over the next few days it would be much easier to list those who did not call upon them than to list those who did. Both Stephen and Liza were overwhelmed with both the generosity and good wishes of their neighbours, and baby and mother continued to progress well.

* * *

Cook had set up the old wooden cradle in one corner of the kitchen, a safe distance away from the hot stoves. This greeted Liza when she returned to work and Damaris was quickly introduced to her new surroundings after being lovingly cuddled and doted upon by the Cook. Constance was sent into the main house to join the Squire's youngest son, 'Love', in his tuition. She was allowed to do this at times but not during the serious teaching of Latin and French. Love was like a brother to Constance, whilst Wrestling was away at school she was his companion in most things that he did. In his free time he played with her and kept her out of harm's way. He often sat and played the clavichord. This seemed to have a mesmerizing effect upon her, and she would just sit upon the floor observing his every movement in utter silence. On occasions, although Constance was really too young, he would sit her up alongside him and encouragingly support her in her efforts to play something. Normally an unrecognisable din would emerge but Love made every effort to sing along to the tune. Constance, still not two years of age, giggled with glee at their attempts and the Lady and the Squire very often rushed in to admire the duet. They saw

Constance as part of the family and admired her beauty and early intelligence. In all of his work Constance made every attempt to copy Love's progress. Whilst this went on Cook made every effort to lighten Liza's workload, insisting that she occasionally put her feet up and show attention to the new offspring. It was also obvious that Cook was trying to slip everything she could into Liza's diet to rebuild her stamina. Liza showed her appreciation but had little need to because Cook loved her dearly.

The Cook's name was Harriet Broad and her husband 'Albert' was the coachman and general dogsbody about the big house. He did everything that no one else would claim responsibility for. He was the Squire's confidante in times of need, companionship and trust. He did general repairs around the house, either keeping everything in good repair for the Squire or advising him upon the proper course of action. Albert often accompanied the Squire away on business, when they would travel to either London, Leeds, York or other important parts. Sometimes both the Lady and Love would travel with them. When they remained at home, Harriet had the honour of being lady companion to her Lady within the household. At these times she would sit more with the Lady and assist her with Love. They would read, knit or sew together and Harriet often encouraged Love in these pursuits whilst she and the Lady discussed generally the way of life.

In the gardens of the big house Stephen and Bill were today pulling turnips and storing them in sacks. Bill stood up to relieve the tension in his back and knees and to wipe the sweat from his brow. He spoke quietly to Stephen, "Both of the Pastors say that the hierarchies been snooping around again lately."

"When was this exactly?"

"Only t'other day."

"They're not s'pecting any more bother, are they?"

"Who knows these days, Stephen? The Squire says that things down in London are getting worse and Pastor Smyth says that one or two have been took in Yorkshire and no one seems to know where to. It's been weeks since they were last seen."

"It's the young un's as I'm afeard for Bill. I don't wants to see Liza left alone to care for her own."

"She never be on her own Stephen, you knows that. We won't let that be happening."

"You know what I mean though, Bill, we gotta take care."

"I thinks we do, Stephen. We gots to keep our wits about us and speak out if we sees out wrong."

Bill stooped back to his labour and Stephen carried a full sack away to the cold store. After emptying its contents he returned to Bill's side. He then set about lifting one of the first potatoes to check the quality.

"I don't know how we ever managed before these Stephen."

"No, Bill but now it's all potato in't it? I sometimes say to Liza, 'We did eat before potatoes yer know', my old Ma and Pa lived most their lives without."

"What's she say ter that then Stephen?"

"She says yer lucky ter eat at all there's plenty that don't, and she's right Bill."

"It's true Stephen. Squire says that there's more on streets in London than has shelter above um and most is begging fer food."

At that moment Cook's voice filled the air as she beckoned to them to come in for a quick break and they knew that there would be hot biscuits waiting for them inside.

* * *

That Sunday, all the villagers were there waiting for Stephen and Liza at the church when their cart trundled into the field. Damaris was finely dressed up in an embroidered christening smock and a pretty little bonnet. It was like one huge family swarming about them, all proud and blessing the child through the Holy Spirit. Inside all instantly stood up and clapped enthusiastically as Liza carried the baby towards the christening font. When the water was dribbled across the baby's tiny forehead everyone cheered and hats were thrown into the air. Pastor Clyfton held her up and showed her off for the entire congregation to see. He had the biggest smile in the church at that moment. The Squire, gesturing towards Stephen, pushed two shiny coins into his hand, 'Fer the babby', he said. Thus repeating the same gesture that he had made at Constance's christening. Stephen nodded and thanked him for his generosity.

After the service was completed, the Pastor stood at the door and spoke individually with each one of them as they left. He spoke to them of the religious persecution that was taking place and the fact that it was far from improving. He also said that he was concerned as to how much longer they would be able to use the church without being censored in some way and he warned that they should be forever cautious.

* * *

Stephen, Bill, William Bradford and the Squire all stood talking outside for a while whilst the womenfolk were cuddling and kissing the baby. Bradford, at the age of 16, was a very intelligent youth and was telling the others of the stories that he had heard of other countries where people were allowed to live their lives free from this constant fear in which they lived; people who had their own beliefs and were not persecuted by others. He spoke to them too of John Robinson, a friend of his family, with whom he had discussed the 'New World'. Word had it, he said, that there were wondrous sights, such as food that they had never seen and riches greater than they would ever know. The Squire said that there were times when he dreamt of living in another place: where they would be free of the fear that they now had and where they needn't hold their tongue for the danger of being hanged.

Later that afternoon, in Broombank cottage, Stephen was telling Liza about the discussion that he and the other menfolk had been having. He admitted that he hadn't got the full grasp of it all, some of it had been beyond his comprehension, but he was afraid that the Squire might be considering a move, uprooting, to foreign parts.

"He won't be doing that Stephen, don't yer fret."

"He was mighty strong on it Liza. I never seen him so worked up about something."

"Harriet tells me that m'lady has spoken of it but she says that the Squire's heart is in Scrooby and that it would be like ripping it out fer him and he'll never leave it."

"Don't yer never dream of elsewhere though Liza, somewhere that's always warmer, somewhere where we has more than we has now and somewhere better fer the young uns?"

"I do that Stephen, but my old Ma, she said be happy with what yer got cus tomorrow yer might have nothing."

"It's very true Liza but we could also have more."

"I got you and I got me little babbies and I got me cottage. I loves Scrooby and I believe that God's blessed us."

Stephen lent forwards and kissed her gently upon her cheek. Smiling at her, he realised she would always be there to rescue him from any dark pit that his mind chose to lose him in and she was forever wiser than him by the bucketful. He lifted her straw basket and inside he found two small corn dollies, one for each of the girls, there was also biscuits, bread and honey. The Cook had passed this basket to Liza as they had climbed back onto their cart outside the church. Stephen's face lit up.

"We got good friends, like family, Liza, and if they ever go anywhere then we'll be going with um."

"We can't do that, Stephen."

"We can and we will!"

"If the Squire goes off to God knows where then he'll find some other helpers, he won't need us."

This met with a deadly silence until Stephen rose to his feet muttering that he was away outside to the well. Liza knew how stubborn Stephen could be at times and she also knew that when he had these ideas, well, he would wrestle with them. He had ideas that she might never entertain but this was why she loved him so much. She loved him but worried for him. She reached into the basket and she pulled out one of the corn dollies. She passed it to Constance, who had been playing quietly upon the floor, and then she nursed the new baby tightly to her breast, thinking on of what might come now of Stephen's ideas.

Chapter Four

Christmas 1607

In the Squire's kitchen, come noon, a small gathering of the regulars had come together for Christmas. These being: the Cook and her husband Albert, their sole child, Natalie, Bill Latham, Stephen, Liza, Constance and Damaris. All except one were gathered around the highly scrubbed, white wooden table. In the centre of which, upon the Squire's pewter, sat a goose. This was neatly trimmed around with potatoes, parsnips and onions. Albert was finely poised and prepared to carve when suddenly the large wooden door swung open. Love ran into the room with a huge jug of punch, as he always did at this time in the year, compliments of his father, the Squire and his lady. Stephen took the heavy jug from Love wondering how he had made it so far in such haste whilst spilling so little. Love, with a huge smile upon his face, then pulled open one of the large dresser drawers. From inside he took out two little parcels, which he said were for Constance and Damaris. He then handed these over to the girl's mother, without saying another word, before rushing out to return from whence he had come. Albert returned his concentration to his task of carving. Cook handed around the platters and Bill poured the punch. Over in the corner of the kitchen, neatly tucked into Harriet's cradle, was baby Damaris. Then the large door swung open and Love's head suddenly re-appeared and he shouted cheerily, "Merry Christmas" before just as suddenly disappearing.

For many years now this small group had gathered in this same way to celebrate the festivities together. The Squire and his wife would take their dinner at 6.00 p.m. usually with their invited guests. This allowed Cook to give her own little dinner, to her guests, at lunchtime. Sufficient time was then available for the kitchen to be cleared and readied in preparation for the evening by 2.00 p.m. Later in the evening, following the dinner, the Squire threw open his doors for all who wished to join the family. These included all of those present now with the Cook and any other villagers with the mind to. All would then join in with the games, and partake of a few drinks, taken in the large sitting room.

During the Cook's lunch all generally exchanged pleasantries and discussed the year's events. This year, events that had been occurring recently influenced their line of conversation. Bill started to tell them about something he and the Pastor had been discussing regarding a new Bible that was being written at this present time; King James was supposedly giving it his own time. The Pastor believed it all to be a waste and that it would simply not change attitudes. He was still concerned with the loss of the church. He believed that unless they could reform, nothing would alter, and he knew that there was no desire to do that.
Albert said, "Since Hampton Court nothing's changed. Far from improving, it's gotten worse."
"They keep threatening to chase us all out and that's what they'll do," added Stephen in a pessimistic tone.
Bill agreed, "The conference changed nothing and James has got no time fer none of us except his own. Squire says that,

'when any members, brave enough that is, dare to speak out in Parliament they're quickly silenced'."

Stephen then asked, "Does the Squire still keep talking about leaving Albert?"

"He says that he's more and more frustrated that they's more intent upon arguing 'divine rights' than running the blasted country, excusing my language. He thinks they got no time fer us country folk. He often talks about the 'New World' and Europe, but he loves Scrooby."

Bill was both angry and annoyed and said, "It's these Bishops have got all the power. They'm a feathering their own nests whilst all t'others are struggling."

"Tis a sure thing that King James has no time fer us," added Bill.

Harriet knocked the table sharply with the soup ladle, bringing them to an abrupt attention.

"Stop it now!" she rasped. "Such talk's not fer the Lord's Day! You's getting all worked up and angry, when we ought to be a celebrating. Let's hear no more such talk of things or you'll get no gooseberry pie."

Liza added, "Hear, hear. We only has Christmas once a year and we should put aside all such things and be happy, enough's enough!"

This outburst well and truly silenced the menfolk, having been rightly put in their places. All went briefly quiet till Stephen added, "'Tis a beautiful punch this year."

The snow outside lay crisp and deep after the second day of continuous snowfall. In contrast the kitchen was snug and warm and the Christmas spirit took hold of them causing them to start with outbursts of Christmas carols and lots of laughter. All sat contented until the time drew near to 2.00 p.m. and the Cook forever dutiful, reminded them all of their responsibilities towards the household. They immediately responded by gathering together the pots and pans, washing up, and clearing the room. Cook went into the cold store pantry and returned with a goose twice the size of that which they had just consumed. She placed it carefully upon the cleared table; then she fetched the herbs and onions in order to commence with the stuffing. Liza and the Cook's daughter had both rolled up their sleeves and were busy at the sink. Bill and Stephen had gone into the yard and were busily chopping firewood for the master's hearth at that evening's feast. Albert had gone to the stables to give the horses their routine check and also to feed them their Christmas carrot treats. The two young children, Constance, who was now three, and Damaris, fifteen months, were both sitting upon the deep window seat watching the snowflakes fall. They both held in their tiny hands the small wooden gifts taken from Love's packages. Liza called to the Cook, "The milk's warm fer the bab."

She took the small black pot from the pothook above the fire and popped her thumb into it. Then she lifted Damaris from the window seat and sat her upon Cook's nursing chair and began carefully spoon-feeding her with the milk. Liza had been finding it increasingly more difficult to suckle the child so she occasionally now used warmed goat's milk.

At 6.00 p.m. with some bread and meat set aside in the kitchen, Stephen and Bill sat with the children. Cook, Natalie and Liza came to and fro between the master's dining room and the kitchen in service to the table. Albert was now at his post inside the dining room, busily serving drinks. Now and again when the women entered the kitchen they picked upon scraps to keep them nourished. Both Liza and Harriet also then made time for the girls giving them little titbits. Albert's food was set to one side within the breadbox until he returned. It would be at about 9.00 p.m. before they were all allowed to join in with the other guests in the sitting room. By now they all knew just what to expect. Love would play for everyone's entertainment upon the clavichord, where he would be accompanied by his elder brother, 'Wrestling', who was presently at home on leave from boarding school. Wrestling had a sweet voice and sang the most perfect Christmas carols, which generally brought tears to one or two eyes. Later they would go on to play party games and maybe dance a little, at least this is what they had done at previous Christmas celebrations. The men would drink the Squire's best apple juice and the ladies would have their own special treats and discuss light-hearted matters.

At nine when the staff entered the room they were greeted firstly by the Squire and his Lady and then by the guests. They were all instantly made to feel a welcome part of the extended family. Stephen and Frances Alden were there with their son John, who was now just turned seven years of age, along with John Carver and his wife Katherine who were up from London. Pastor Clyfton was also present. John Carver had been a very good friend of the Squire's since early days, as both their fathers had been before them. Brewster suggested that the men should retire to the library, as was the custom, directly after dinner. They then did this, thus leaving the women and the children to their own devices. Carver immediately started to tell the others about his recent visit to Amsterdam, where he had been on business. He paused to ask the Squire if he could now have the box that he had been stored for him. Brewster acknowledged that he could and asked if Albert would mind collecting it from his bureau. This was collected and placed safely into Carver's waiting hands. He slowly unwrapped the package and carefully pulled out an assortment of cleverly designed clay pipes. Some were slightly fancier than the others but all drew the attention of the admiring and inquisitive onlookers. He then withdrew a pouch and began to pack the brown fibred contents slowly and meticulously into the pipes. This brought some comment from the men. Once completed, Carver passed one of the finest carved pipes to Brewster, who handled it with care. Having then taken one for himself he handed around the rest. He asked if Albert might fetch a lighted taper from the fireside and heads were tilted with interest. Of course the Squire had previously been witness to this practice (having seen it before upon his travels, but he had never partaken of it). Albert also knew exactly what was going to happen next, but the others were baffled. Having received the taper, Carver slowly commenced to light up the pipes, doing his own first to give the example. He then lit the Squire's pipes, attending to his and then the other gents in turn. Pastor Clyfton was last in the line and he, having seen the process commence and then witnessed the coughing and spluttering that followed, gracefully declined the offer and handed the pipe back to Carver. Bill and the Squire immediately seemed to grasp the ability, drawing deeply upon the pipes and emitting great clouds of fluffy smoke. They each laughed at one another and then asked several questions of Carver about this new substance, concerning its origin and use, to which he responded in turn. It raised much interest and amusement within the group, and their ears perked up when Carver told them that, 'King James had taken such a distaste to the use of tobacco and that he was clearly at odds with his courtiers'.

The conversation slowly turned back towards Amsterdam, with Bill and Stephen enquiring of its whereabouts. Carver informed them that it was the capital city of Holland in Europe. Squire Brewster enquired about its finer points, if it had any. To this Carver replied, 'it has many'. Squire Brewster had actually been there seven years or so earlier but wished to know if it had changed over these years. Carver replied, 'it is much the same and that in my humble opinion it is a fine city, a wondrous place'. He suggested that the Squire might do the honour of joining him upon his next need to visit. The Squire said that he would very much like to do that. Pastor Clyfton then opened up a discussion regarding the religious beliefs of that country, to which Carver stated that he had witnessed no oppression there. He said that he had found a far greater freedom there to practise in whatever beliefs one might wish to express without fear of persecution. Then Pastor Smyth said that it would be wonderful to have the freedom to praise the Lord freely without Royal prescription. Carver reminded the Squire that they shared a mutual friend in the city who had been involved in the emigration of others who had left this country. His name was Sir Edwyn Sandys. Brewster said that this was true and that he must look up Sir Edwyn in the next two weeks that he was to be in London because he had not seen him for some twelve months. Carver suggested that they should all take lunch together as he was due to be there at Easter with the family. He said that he would confirm the details with Sir Edwyn at a later date.

All of the party at the Squire's home shared the same religious disposition and none of them gave any favour whatsoever towards the King's stance and indeed the rigidity and enforcement that prevailed. They were all in agreement that the persecution had become obsessive and that there were some Bishops who actively supported the physical punishment upon those who actually offended, or in 'their views' offended. Some of these so-called offenders were more able and, indeed, more committed to the cause and the spreading of the Gospel than those Bishops had ever been. Following these discussions, and the resolution to which they had reached, the party of gentlemen resumed their positions alongside their good ladies and the children within the sitting room. Pastor Clyfton immediately took up his position at the clavichord striking off with a full-hearted rendition of a carol. All enthusiastically joined in and picked up upon the festive cheer; enjoying each other's company, laughing and joking, eating and drinking. It was to be four days later before the weather had improved sufficiently to allow the Carvers and the Aldens to take their leave of the kind hearted generosity of their hosts. Then both families shared a coach leaving the Manor to depart for their own homes, thus leaving Scrooby to recover from its extended Christmas and to return to some normality.

Chapter Five

Easter 1608

With the Squire and his family away in the city their home was left in an almost ghostly silence. The Cook and Natalie left behind without a husband and father, felt like tiny pebbles in a huge barrel. Harriet continued with her daily chores intending not to lose her daily routine, but now she was just providing for Natalie, the Hopkins's, Bill and herself. Stephen and Bill continued their toil outside in the gardens, whilst Liza, Damaris and Constance moved about the big house cleaning and dusting. The girls both missed Love but their mother tried to keep them occupied with one little task or another. This was difficult to achieve with two such young girls but Liza did not wish for them to be a burden to others. There were times in the day when Damaris was still laid down to sleep and without hesitation Cook would keep a diligent eye upon her lying within the old cradle. Occasionally she would need to comfort her if she cried out, and Harriet would settle her by drawing her high stool alongside the crib and singing a sweet lullaby. It had been many years now since her own daughter, Natalie, had occupied the crib but she was well practised with Liza's. She started to rock the crib and to sing gently, starting with a muffled hum and then developing into—

"Alieu, Alieu, Mama's little ala bala coo
Hush a bye, rock a bye
Mama's little baby
Mama's little ala bala coo."

Damaris's mouth creased at the corners and slowly, with eyes tightly closed, she would begin to smile. This generally brought a tear to Harriet's eyes. Then she would gently pat Damaris and continue to sing. Inevitably, this brought another little smile and the teardrop would run gently down Harriet's cheek. She told herself not to be so silly, scolding herself beneath her breath, whilst she continued gently to rock the crib. In her mind she pictured young Dorothy lying there. Harriet's second born daughter had only survived for six months. Although her name was Dorothy, Albert called her 'Dotty'. Harriet had had difficulties throughout her pregnancy and a very difficult and extended labour. When Dotty was finally born she was blue in the face, starved of oxygen, due to the umbilical chord being wrapped tightly around her tiny throat. Both Albert and Marion Huggins fought to release her but she never really thrived after that. Her little life had been one immense struggle and finally she had died, silently six months later, in Harriet's loving arms. For years after this Harriet too had also wanted to die and had it not been for Natalie's needs and Albert's love she would have taken her own life.

"Mrs Broad, Mrs Broad!"
Harriet was suddenly startled by Constance's shrill tones. Her little voice split the air and shook Harriet from her dreams; she jumped nervously. Looking down at Damaris she realised that she was now fast asleep.
"Oh, what is it my lovely?"
"It's me Ma missus, she says can you come?"
"Yes child, where is she?"

Constance clasped hold firmly of Harriet's short chubby fingers and led her away from the kitchen. Harriet was Broad by name and broad by nature and she waddled gently behind the girl. Constance led her up the master's stairs and Harriet had to pause now and again, puffing and blowing. When they reached the master's chambers, Harriet immediately recognised the need for haste. Liza was struggling at the foot of the four-poster bed, of which one leg had come adrift. Her face was red and she beckoned Harriet to help quickly.

"Oh my word! God save us! What are yer doing me, lass?"

"It's the leg, Harriet. It gave way on me. I can't hold on ter this much longer."

Harriet stooped low and caught hold of the bed.

"I'll hold it lass. You put it back."

Liza pushed hard upon the turned polished leg whilst Harriet puffed and wheezed. Suddenly it snapped back into place.

"There it goes lass," groaned Harriet, with immense relief.

"Best get Bill to take a look at it later, just in case."

Both of the women sat back upon the edge of the bed, catching their breath.

"It's a bloomin heavy bed, that is."

"It is that, lass. Perhaps yer should come and take yer break now. I wants to talk with yer anyhow."

They all descended the wide staircase together. Harriet had a tight grip upon the banister with her right hand and with her other hand she had a tight grip of Constance. Liza was on the other side firmly holding Constance's hand. Having their feet now soundly upon the white flag floor they turned towards the kitchen door. Liza went immediately to Damaris to check that no harm had come to her whilst she had been alone. She was still soundly asleep. Constance ran out into the yard beyond, trying to locate both her father and Bill in order to tell them about the master's bed.

Cook and Liza sat together at the kitchen table. Before them was a boiled egg especially made for the Easter time. Liza asked Harriet what was so urgent upon her mind.

"Oh, it aint urgent Liza, it's just that I wanted to tell someone abouts what my Albert's been saying."

"Albert? What's he said Hatty?"

"Well, he's been telling me that the Squire's seriously considering leaving England."

"Leaving England? No, he can't, Cook, it's not true, surely it aint, is it?"

"That's what I says Liza, but he says it is."

"But where, I mean, where would he go?"

"He don't say that Liza, he just says that's what he's thinking and that's what he's talking abouts in London."

"Stephen told me about them talking. I mean him and that Mr Carver."

"Yes, well, that's who he'll be a seeing and that Sir, you know, Mr Sandys, whom they mention?"

"Oh, I remembers, Stephen also said that they were a talking a mighty lot abouts Amsterdam or at least something like that."

"Amsterdam, is it? When did Stephen say all this Liza?"

"After Christmas dinner, you know, when all the men-folk got together."

"What's so special abouts Amsterdam then?"

"Oh, I don't know that, but master must see something in it."

"I don't know what we'd all do if master went and upped sticks."

"No, Stephen says that too, but he also says that he'll go too."

"He wouldn't, would he? I mean, you wouldn't would you?"

"Stephen won't need asking twice and when he's a mind to then he takes some budging."

"Oh, my words, I don't know what I'd do."

"Well, we've all had enough of this religious bother and Stephen says he wants a better life fer the kids and me, but I says, well I loves my Broombank cottage."

Liza looked a little perplexed and concerned with all this talk. Harriet realised and said, "Don't yer fret wench, it'll all be fine. I knows it will."

"I hopes yer right Hatty, I do truly. I prays to God it'll be."

* * *

Meanwhile, in the London offices of Sir Edwin Sandys, (Treasurer of the London Company), Sir Edwin was busily discussing patents with John Carver and William Brewster. The three gentlemen sat in winged chairs, each relaxed with a small tot of wine in his hands. Edwin was explaining that:

"The Warwick patents will entitle you to settle the land legally, this being in either of two parts of the Company's Northern jurisdiction." He went on to say, "This is how the first settlers have organised things and word has just been received only yesterday that at this very moment they are busy building a new life in Jamestown and that all fairs well."

Brewster butted in, "Yes, that's all well and good Edwin but I will not go that far. As we have said I have been giving some real consideration of late to Holland but not the Americas. Anyway, it might not come to that, but we shall see."

"At this time we won't be ruling anything out Edwin. I'll talk some more to William but both of us wish to thank you for your good offices and your kind words of guidance." Carver added, "Let's not be too ready to dismiss things, William."

"Oh no, I wouldn't do that, thank you, Edwin, but as you say, John, this all needs careful consideration."

There were a few moments of silence as they all sipped from their drinks. Then Brewster added, "It's Scrooby see. It's like one huge family. It's my life and it means more to me than anything. Scrooby's in my blood but I know deep down in my soul that when it comes to a decision, well, me and the other Coreligionists, we'll all be of one mind."

Sandys admired Brewster immensely; he also admired the people of Scrooby. He could see that William had something close to his heart, something that he did not have. He admired them all for what they stood for. He was fully aware of the risks that they were taking. He was isolated in his ivory tower, adrift from real life. This conjured up something within his own heart and he felt a sudden spurt of youth about him. He assured William that if they needed support of any kind then he must not hesitate to ask.

"Anything within my power. If it can be done, then it will be." Carver sat back speechless and contented within his comfortable chair. Sandys leant forward and replenished their wine.

There was something about Sandy's attitude that had an immediate effect upon Carver and he suddenly said, "You know, William, I like the people of Scrooby; I have always felt at home upon my visits there. I feel as welcome there as I do within my own home and the folk treat me as their own. They've always made me truly welcome and just at this moment, well, I tell you, I'm a mind to come with you all wherever you go."

Sir Edwin chuckled, "You'd do that, John?"

"You know Edwin, I think I would and now that it's occurred to me I'd be mighty happy to."

William sat ashen-faced suddenly realising the gravity of his actions; he had the look of a man with the death sentence being announced.

John Carver saw his face, studied him for a while, and then asked, "What is it William, what troubles you?"

"It's suddenly occurred to me that this is probably the most serious decision that I may ever make in my life and that maybe I overestimate our allegiance. I mean, will Scrooby stand by me? I could never leave them, I know I couldn't."

Edwin suddenly bemused said, "Why on earth would you do it, William? You won't need to and even I feel it, they'd follow you man for man to the ends of the earth and you know it. If you go, then they'll all go."

"I can't speak for the others, Edwin, that's what I've suddenly realised is that they have their homes and loyalties and I respect them all."

Carver could understand William's concerns but he knew that they were unfounded. He also knew that it was William's respect for those that he loved that stopped him from taking them for granted, but Sir Edwin was right.

"You know that they'd follow you anywhere, William. You know it in you're heart and I know it too."

All three sat back once more with these thoughts in their minds, while the light of the candles slowly flickered across their faces, and the logs burning upon the hearth cast shadows about the office. William's face slowly melted, returning to its former flush and then a sudden beam.

"That's it!" he cried, "I'll do it and I'll take the lot of them. I'll talk to them all. God wants this for us, I know that he does. This is God-sent, a new beginning, a new start in life, a new adventure. I hate to say it but this country that I dearly love is stagnant. Politicians sit chewing the cud. The King spends all his time hunting. They pay not a scrap of attention to what this country and its people really desire. They'd rather persecute than to listen. They're all too wrapped up in their own kind than to see what's happening to this country."

"Well," said John, "never a truer word was spoken and never by a finer man. If you do it, then I'll do it too, you know you're right, and you're too loyal to damn this land, but I say let this land be damned. Why not start afresh?"

* * *

The following afternoon John Carver stood beside the Brewster's coach wishing each and everyone a safe journey home to Nottingham. Albert sat perched on high above the luggage chests and with respect he nodded to Mr Carver.

"You'll be in touch soon then, William?"

"I will be John, that I will, and thank you for your support. God bless you and yours."

"And God go with you, William."

He tipped his hat towards the coach and smiled upon Lady Brewster and their younger son. The coach jolted and creaked forward as the horses snatched and the wheels began rolling gently. John slowly waved them away.

Chapter Six

'Scrooby's Choice

Back safely in Scrooby, with a good night's rest behind them, William sent urgently for the Pastor Clyfton. Albert carried the message to the church where he found the Pastor busily tending his roses.

"Pastor!"

"Oh, how goes it with you Albert, when did you arrive home?"

"Late last evening, Pastor. The master has sent me upon urgent instructions to fetch you to him."

"What's all the urgency Albert is something amiss?"

"I don't know Pastor but master might say it be and he must talk with yer."

The Pastor stood his muddy spade against the stone church wall, wiped his hands upon a length of sacking, and scraped his boots off with a trowel. Now well prepared, both he and Albert started away from the church towards the great house, side by side. The Pastor enquired of the Squire's mood and health as they strolled.

"How was London, Albert? Was the weather good there?"

"Yes, both were fine after the early mists had lifted."

"Was the trip enjoyable, then?"

"Yes, very much so Pastor."

The Pastor tried gently to tease the smallest bit of information from Albert to try to ascertain the master's mood, but he drew little from it.

"Did you have trouble on the road, Albert?"

"No Pastor there was no trouble. All went well."

"Does the master seem; I mean to say, is he a worried man?"

"No sir, he isn't."

"And her Lady, Albert, and young Love, are they well too?"

"Yes Pastor. I don't know why he wants yer so urgent like, but he said to bring yer with haste."

By now they had reached the large studded front door, which was ajar and creaked as Albert pushed it aside, allowing the Pastor to pass by him. There was a call and suddenly the Squire's head rounded the study doorway.

"Is that you Pastor?"

"It is," was the Pastor's reply.

"I'm in the study Pastor and ask Albert to join us please."

The Pastor turned and beckoned Albert to accompany him from the hallway and through into the study. They both entered to find the master standing before the hearth with the fire burning warmly within it. The Squire took a seat and asked them both to join him. It was a cosy setting before the log fire with the sparks jumping above the twist of the flames lighting up the darkness of the flue. The Pastor sensed no troubles.

"I needed to talk with you Pastor," began the Squire.

The Pastor immediately began to repeat the enquiries of the lane – how was the master's health, had they had a good journey and so on. But the Squire abruptly ended this conversation, wishing to speak bluntly of his own concerns.

"In London I had a meeting with Sir Edwin Sandys."

This brought forth a further interruption by the Pastor who then began to enquire of Sir Edwin's well being.

"He's well enough Pastor. Please could you try not to interrupt. I need to say this now, if you'll pardon me."

The Pastor just nodded graciously.

"John Carver was also there with us and we discussed in earnest the present state of the country."

Albert nodded, "'Tis true, 'tis a state."

The Pastor just mumbled incoherently.

"Well," he continued, "Sir Edwin got to explaining that there are wonderful opportunities for those adventurers amongst us, good opportunities and better living in other countries."

The Pastor now suddenly felt a need to intervene.

"Oh Squire, 'tis as I feared – rumour has it that you would leave the village."

"I would that," the Squire replied showing little emotion.

The Pastor was taken aback, totally shocked.

"This village of Scrooby, this of your ancestor's birth, the village and all your friends?"

"No, listen I says, let me finish. It could be a new start for all of us."

All become silent. The Pastor studied the Squire's face. He looked deep into his eyes and his soul. Then he turned toward Albert looking for some sort of reaction. Albert looked as dumbfounded as he himself felt.

"All of us?" he asked.

"Yes, all of us."

Again a deathly silence fell. Then the Pastor spoke.

"I have to go where my calling takes me."

The Squire asked, "How about if it calls from Holland?"

The Pastor thought again for a moment and then replied.

"If it calls from Holland, then I'll go."

"How about you, Albert?" the Squire asked.

"I think Harriet and I are too old fer all of that wandering master."

"But would you consider it? Please say that you would."

"I'll speaks to Harriet, but I don't know sir."

"Anyway," said the Squire, looking again to the Pastor,

"It's grand to be back and I wants to speak to all t'others about what I've proposed."

He then asked of the Pastor, "Can we arrange to speak to the 'family' as soon as possible? I'd like to explain thoroughly my ideas to every one of them."

The Pastor replied, "Yes, of course, it needs to come from you personally. I'll get the word about but I'm sure you're aware of just how cautious we all need to be?"

All three rose as one and walked through into the hallway. Albert said his leave and left them to exit by the back door. The Pastor and the Squire paused a moment at the front entrance. Then the Pastor again asked, "Are you sure about all of this William?"

"Yes, I believe I am," he replied, and the Pastor said his goodbyes.

Albert stood in the kitchen, contemplating, whilst at the same time considering Harriet's present mood. He wanted so much to ask her here and now. Harriet was fully aware of his hovering and waited impatiently.

"Have you got time to stand about now, Albert? If there's something on yer mind then get it off will yer."

Just at that moment, Stephen cried out for Albert to come to him outside, and so Albert said nothing. He simply passed through the kitchen and out through the rear door into the yard. Stephen was standing twenty feet or so away and he beckoned for Albert to follow him. Albert caught up with him along the pathway.

"What is it, Stephen? What's so urgent?"

"One of the sheep's in breech and I needs a hand afore we lose her."

Albert followed Stephen through the lower field and into the little sheepfold. There lay one of the sheep in the hay, obviously in difficulty, kicking with her back legs.

"You get the warm soapy water Stephen."

"'Tis already here Albert."

Stephen passed the pail closer to Albert's reach and then he put a calming hand to the sheep's side.

"Where's Bill?" asked Albert.

"He's been sent upon some urgent errand fer master."

"We'll just have to manage then; you takes hold of the legs and keep them apart."

Stephen did just as he was told. Albert had a vast experience in these matters, more so than Stephen.

With a warmly washed soapy hand, Albert penetrated the ewe, firstly with his fingers and then his hand, feeling for the limbs of the lamb. Limbs were flailing about internally and Albert patiently sought for a flailing foot. One came to his grasp and he caught it firmly teasing it gently upon its way; he quickly tied off a length of twine to it. He tried once more and following the length of the limb he could feel its little tail. He caught hold easing it to and fro, gently pulling the tail and the twine towards this world. Gradually it appeared into the light. Albert adjusted his grip to the base of the tail and the leg. Just then the ewe twisted upwards catching Stephen unaware, and for a moment, Albert believed he would lose his grip. Stephen took a firmer grip holding both the body and the head of the sheep closely to the ground. Albert grew concerned, but suddenly the tail was back within his fingers. Slowly, but surely, the tail re-emerged and then the hind.

"Depends on t'other rear leg now, Stephen."

But as quickly as these words had left his mouth the ewe again heaved and out shot the lamb, the other rear leg along its breast, with all of its bloodied fetal membranes behind it. Albert took it fully into his lap and Stephen quickly rubbed the lamb down with handfuls of hay. Both of the men drew a long sigh of relief whilst Albert pulled away slowly from it and tried to remove as much as he could from his clothing with the warm soapy water. Getting his clothes into such a state was not going to be a good way of improving Harriet's mood. Now how could he approach the subject of his master's proposals with her?

"How did the journey go then Albert?"

"Oh, without a problem Stephen. Just tiring, you know?"

Albert took a cloth from his pocket and mopped his brow, he then continued.

"But master's come back with a problem."

"How d'yer mean, Albert?"

"Well, I suppose it could be seen as a problem, but it's more like these sort of, well, wondrous ideas."

"How d'yer mean, 'wondrous ideas'?"

"Well, I s'pose you'll be finding out soon enough, as will everyone, he's talking about us all uprooting and, if he has it his way, going off somewhere foreign."

"How d'yer mean, 'us all'?"

"As I say, he intends talking to all the village soon enough, but anyways, it seems that in London while he was with Mr Carver and Sir Edwin they were talking about 'the New World' as master puts it. Master's got all these big ideas about how wondrous it might all be. He call it, 'the promise of paradise'. It seems that they discussed the Americas but master is going on about 'Amsterdam'."

"Amsterdam is it, Albert? But why Amsterdam?"

"You remembers at Christmas, Stephen, how Mr Carver was going on about Amsterdam and you remember that tobacco? Well, anyway, master believes we would be away from the turmoil but still close enough to home. He could continue his business, couldn't he?"

"But why should we all go?"

"We don't have to, do we? But, the threats here to us all are becoming too great. He's not a happy man, is he? He says we're a family and he really believes it. He doesn't really want to go anywhere, does he? I mean, his heart's in Scrooby, but it might come to it."

"It's not surprising really, is it, Albert, now that you think about it, well is it? While you were away news came to the village that one of the Puritans further north had had his entrails ripped from his body and was carted about the local villages as a warning to us all."

"No, Stephen! That's truly awful! I know they keep going on about the pond duckings, and the stocks, and the like, but that is awful. Does master know that yet?"

"I don't know, Albert, I've not yet spoken with him but you can see his reasoning. He's an intelligent man, is master."

"I got to speak to Harriet but we're old, Stephen. It's not like it is fer you and Liza."

"How would we do it anyway, Albert? How could we? What would happen to Scrooby?"

"The Squire just sent me urgently fer the Pastor and I just sat with them while they discussed it. Pastor's going to arrange so that he can talks to everyone."

"Will yer speak to Harriet then?"

"'Course I will but I just don't know how to do it or how she'll take it. I was about to try just now when you calls me urgently."

"Liza loves our little cottage and she loves this village; she don't believe that grass is always greener on t'other side, I don't know how she'll be with it."

Stephen offered the little lamb to its mother's head and she lovingly licked upon its face. He placed it gently by her side and then both men raised from their haunches. Stephen picked up the pail and both men walked slowly together back up the field. Stephen left Albert at the stable door and Albert continued on back into the kitchen. Here he found that Liza was now at the kitchen table, feeding Constance and Damaris, whilst Harriet had her hands in the sink.

Albert nodded to Liza and patted both the girls upon their heads. He then went and stood alongside Harriet at the sink.

"We need to speak privately," he said.

Harriet looked at him, rather surprised as they kept few secrets from each other, but Albert looked very earnest in his mood. She wiped her hands and wandered across into the larder and Albert trailed behind her. Harriet stopped in the middle of the room and then turned about.

"I knew something troubled yer. I asked yer before what it was and you goes dashing off."

"I had too, Harriet. You heard how urgently Stephen called me."

"Yer not ill, are yer?"

"No, woman, listen, will yer, it's master."

"He's not ill, is he?"

"Ohhh! Yer not listening, woman."

All went quiet; it was not often that Harriet saw Albert in such a mind.

"Master's thinking about leaving village."

"No, he can't be. Why would he do that?"

"Listen, 'cus he says things are getting worse and becoming too dangerous round here. We're defying the authorities, yer know and just now Stephen told me something awful."

"Oh, I know all that, but that's north, that's not here."

"No, but it soon could be, anyway, master said we should go to Holland, Harriet?

"'Holland'? We should go?"

"Yes, Holland and all of us."

"You sure about all this, Albert; who knows about it?"

"Well, Stephen does 'cus I just told him and Pastor does 'cus I just had to fetch him to house and I just sat there while they discussed it."

"Holland?"

"Yes, Holland – Amsterdam. He discussed it all in London with Mr Carver and Mr Sandys."

"You say Stephen knows, but Liza knows nothing of it?"

"That's true and you need to leave it to Stephen to talk with Liza himself."

"Oh, I will but she'll be none too pleased."

"I know that too and it's between Stephen and Liza, like it's between me and you. If I were you I'd keep well out of it, 'tis none of our business."

It wasn't until that night, at home in their little cottage, that Stephen dared venture upon the subject with Liza. He tried not to overstate what the possible outcome might be. He tried to deal with it simply as gossip. Liza dealt with the news in much the same way that Harriet had, but she also was very forthright in her opinion; 'she would not go'.

"But what would become of us, Liza?"

"I don't know. I s'pose we'd live on, but I won't leave my little home and I won't drag my little babbies halfway around the world to some foreign land or other."

She was adamant and refused to discuss the matter any further with Stephen even though he told her that all of the village would leave them behind. He told her that they would have to give this greater consideration than she had done. If the master went through with his plans then where would that leave them – high and dry.

All she could say was that they would both have to deal with that situation should the need ever arise and that it probably never would. She said that the master would think better of this before the week was out and all would be back to normal. Stephen finished by shouting, "Then yah don't know the master then, do yer?"

Of course Stephen was right. The master did not think better of it and the word was spread throughout that week that following the Sunday service there would be a public meeting.

* * *

Gilbert and Edward Winslow carried the message from village to village within the local area and, in fact, to all of those in support of Scrooby and the Coreligionists. Gilbert rode everywhere upon Satan, to the most isolated areas and over the furthest distances, whilst his brother Edward used the Winslow's trap to get to the others. All would most likely have been at the Sunday service anyway, but the Squire wanted everyone to be aware that this was no ordinary service and that he had urgent business with them. Both brothers, although being informed of the business agenda, had been asked not to discuss it with anyone. They had been told that enquiries should be politely dismissed thus leaving it entirely to the Squire to state his case and it was hoped to avoid any unworthy speculation. Both brothers were the soul of discretion. Anyone who enquired was told that the Squire had urgent need to speak personally to everyone and that Sunday would reveal all. John Carver had been informed of the Squire's intention and he arrived in the village on Saturday early enough to be able to take luncheon at the Manor. Carver's wife Katherine also accompanied him.

On Sunday morning the church was full to overflowing and because of this it was a spectacular spiritual occasion, with so many praising the lord and singing His hymns that His presence was felt moving amongst them. Right at the front sat the Squire and his family accompanied by John and Katherine Carver. All of the Winslows sat together, whilst the Hopkins's, Albert and his wife and daughter were assembled in another group. The Aldens were there with their son John, as were the Mullings and the Bradfords and many, many more. When the main service drew to a close Pastor Clyfton stepped down and offered his pulpit to both William and John. William started off by addressing the congregation as his friends and family. He thanked them for their attendance and then without delay he began to set out his proposals before them. At times there were audible gasps as some began to grasp the severity of that which he now suggested. It is true that there was unrest within the community and everyone was aware of the persecution that was occurring but many had never dreamt of the extremity of these proposals to which William's intentions had now led. There was a great deal of shuffling and murmuring inside the hall as William stepped aside for Carver to address everyone. He immediately brought them back to attention and expressed, in no few words, his undying support for a man who not only loved the village in which he lived but also the people of that village. He stated that William was a highly principled man and that he had never met another of his kind. He said that if William had reached the decision to which he believed he had then the people should stand at his side and give him their support. Because William always supported them and, this being no exception, he 'always' had the best intentions for Scrooby within his heart. No man could have received any higher accolade of that which Carver gave to William that day and all stood within that hall to acknowledge it. To endorse his support he then expressed his own and his wife's personal intentions: if the people of Scrooby were to accept them as their own, to follow William to wherever it was he finally decided that they should go. Carver then gave way once more to the Squire who thanked him for 'those words of support'. Brewster was also no mean speaker; he was a

Cambridge graduate and a founder member of this particular separatist movement in 1606. Everyone had the greatest respect for him and his family. He was at this time forty-one years of age and as such was also one of the elders of their church. He told the congregation that there was not a man amongst them who would not be given the opportunity to express his own feelings to him in person and that anyone amongst them would be, and had always been, welcome in his house. He said that he would accept every individual decision that was made, understand their reasoning and bear no malice. He then went on to inform them that it was, through one means or another, his own intentions to personally raise the funds that would finance any such moves that they made, if that were to be the majority decision, and that he very much hoped that it would be.

There was a short silence and then a stirring within the congregation; they were both shocked and surprised at the Squire's generous offer. Then there were some dissenting voices; some of the Winslow boys, in particular Josiah and Kenelm, seemed dead-set against any such notion that they should be uprooted from their present way of living and lose the farm that had passed down through the generations of their family. Others contemplated their own fate. Should they happen to be left behind, for instance, how might it affect those who lived in tied cottages? Both Liza and Harriet held their tongues but both were evidently aware of one another's consternation. John Carver, eight years junior to William, was visibly aglow with his sense of adventure and the atmospherics of the moment. He shouted for the crowd to take a motion upon the subject there and then. He wanted a measure of the initial support although he understood only too well the way in which this had shook the village. The crowd responded to his request and unbelievably there were immediately two thirds of those present who raised their hands in support. Another buzz of excitement filled the hall and the doubting Thomases amongst them began to re-evaluate their situation. But then William stepped in once more and suggested that the enormity of any such decision meant that a period of reflection might be advantageous so that due consideration could be given to his proposals. He would then make arrangements, perhaps within a few days, for an initial list to be compiled, and that any such list would be kept open for a period of time after this.

Once outside the church they stepped immediately into a throng of jostling men, women and children all discussing the same matter; some in heated exchanges and others displaying an over exuberance of enthusiasm. Pastors Clyfton and Smyth were the last to leave along with William and John. The small group was immediately joined by William Bradford. The eighteen year old eagerly grasped at each of their hands. Addressing the Squire, he asked whether he could be of some service concerning arrangements or organising that would need to be carried out. He stated that not only did he offer his assistance but also he hoped that he too might be included in the Squire's plans. Bradford's enthusiasm flowed and he made an immediate impression upon William. The Squire had already formed an admiration for the lad for his services within the community and for the commitment that he had always shown towards their religious cause. His response therefore came as such:

"Thank you William. How would you like to spend some time with us at the Manor? There will be much to be done and I'm certain that you will be of great help to us. Speak to your family and then if they agree, rather than you travelling here daily, you would be most welcome to stay with us whilst we are considering all of the details and making the arrangements."

Just then, Edward Winslow came up to them. Edward was the eldest of the five Winslow brothers, and having overheard part of the previous conversation, wished also to offer his services and to pledge his support. The Squire enquired of the rest of the family having formed the notion when inside the hall that some were far less enthusiastic than he appeared to be. Edward replied that no matter what the final decision of the family was, he and his wife would definitely like to be considered.

Some of the congregation returned to the Manor in order to continue their discussions. John Carver needed to make the return trip to London on the following day, so it was urgent that he should be made aware of anything he could achieve within the city to hasten their plans. In particular, he needed to discuss the financial details with William and the others. He would take their plans to Sir Edwin in order to determine what assistance he might offer. Whilst one very organised meeting took place inside the library another smaller, less organised, group met within the kitchen. Some still needed to air their differences and to consider either their opposition or support. Liza was still adamant that she would not go. However, Albert, Harriet and Natalie had resigned themselves to the inevitability of going. Without the Squire's presence in Scrooby they had no home or position there. Now they were left only to consider the speed of which everything was happening; this being too rapid for them. To add to the now fraught atmosphere between Stephen and Liza both of their girls now cried loudly and simultaneously. Natalie did her utmost to offer comfort to Constance and Stephen picked up Damaris and placed her across his shoulder. He walked away from Liza and out through the door into the yard placing himself firmly down upon the stone bench. Liza gave him a few minutes before joining him. Then she sat down beside him, neither of them speaking. Damaris had now settled down, with Stephen comforting her, by patting her gently on her shoulders. He began to rock her gently to and fro. Liza stared at Stephen as if to see into his heart and mind as he swayed gently. Her eyes swelled with tears and she said, "We'll be left all alone."

Stephen replied, "Yes, but where will we be left?"

"How do yer mean, 'where'?"

"Can we depend upon having our little cottage if the master sells out?"

There was a new pause.

"You really think we should go, don't you?"

"Truthfully, Liza, yes, but I won't go anywhere without my family."

There was another pause and then Liza, with tears now trickling gently down her cheeks, leant forward and softly kissed Stephen upon his lips.

"I love you, Stephen."

There was no reply and then she said, "If we must, we must."

"You mean that you'd go?"

"It'd be like our whole family leaving us behind, wouldn't it? So let's do it."

Stephen said, "It will be better fer the children too."

"I know. I don't know what I was thinking. Come back in, let's tell the others."

So they returned into the kitchen and upon breaking the news they were warmly embraced by both Harriet and Albert.

Chapter Seven

Dutch Courage

Throughout the next few weeks the usually sleepy village became a hive of activity as the intensity grew. The normal humdrum of life continued but now it was accompanied by a constant drive towards achieving the goal that had been set at the church meeting. Meetings took place daily in various venues and there were noticeable clusters and gatherings of small groups about the village. Meetings were held regularly at the Manor and messages were carried from here with regularity to London. William Bradford proved to be a willing workhorse at Brewster's beck and call. He started and continued to develop the list of those with enough courage and desire to follow the Squire's lead. Edward Winslow was his very able assistant using up any available time that he could spare from the farm in order to move matters forwards. He continued to do much of the travelling out and about in the peripheries discussing and consulting and carrying back information. Shortly after their decision the congregation had been forced out of the church that now stood barred to all. So subsequent meetings were held either in or outside the Manor according to weather conditions. Those who either decided against the move or were indecisive listened intently to the arguments that were regularly laid out before them.

Shortly after the London meeting, Sir Edwin Sandys travelled to Scrooby with John Carver. He was still behind the initiative that had been shown and intended to encourage Brewster, but he also lobbied him constantly to take the Americas move rather than be solely intent upon going to Holland. There were many benefits to an American move mainly through financial sponsorship, but the Squire had now his mind set upon the local option. Sandys returned to the city with John Carver accepting the resolutions of Brewster and inspired by his leadership. He would try to support them in any manner available now, although Europe limited his options. William found himself having to be the complete diplomatic being both persuasive and encouraging. He took the lead and provided the inspiration that proved useful in many of his discussions, especially if he faced any remaining pockets of opposition. A rift had developed in the Winslow household over the difficulties that they would have to face in running the family farm with some members of the family intent on leaving whilst others opposed their decision. Edward and Gilbert had decided that they would definitely go. John remained in two minds but Josiah and Kenelm were totally opposed to it and became very disillusioned about their prospects.

These were, of course, people who very rarely ever ventured beyond the village boundaries. The local community was their world. Few lived to any late age in life and their entire happiness revolved around family, friends and village. In fact, only a minority of them had received sufficient education and so lacked the ability to enable them to appreciate their predicament. Without the Squire and his able helpers the idea of such events occurring would have been ludicrous. Those intent upon the venture supported and trusted the Squire with their lives. Without his financial backings the majority would not have had the means. William was a man of stone, a determined man, who was driven constantly onwards by those whom he loved. He was determined to seek out for the group a better, safer life, where their religious practices were not condemned and where they would be able to live their lives without this constant threat hanging over them.

Throughout this period William constantly received information of his business contracts from London and elsewhere. It was all too important that he let nothing slip with this great financial commitment that he now had to face. He took greater interest in any news that arrived in England from the first colonisers of Jamestown, but reports were hard to come by. However, the latest rumours were that the resident natives and the extreme conditions were threatening its existence. This news confirmed to him that at the moment he was right to stand by the choice that he had made. Concerns closer to home grew with the intense pressure upon the Puritans and it became increasingly difficult to meet in the Manor. Brewster insisted that every person should watch his tongue, keeping a close counsel for only those whom they knew and trusted. The amount of callers that arrived at the manor daily from outside of the local community increased daily and Brewster was forever concerned that some action might be taken before they could complete their plans. The logistics of the whole enterprise were incredible: how to transfer a complete community across the North Sea and into a foreign land whilst maintaining everyday security and survival. Of even more concern was how to achieve this and not bring the powers of authority crashing down upon them. This appeared regularly upon the agendas of the many meetings that were held. Although John Carver spent much of this period away from the village, William took every possible opportunity available to him to consult with the man he most trusted.

After much deliberation it was decided that the safest plan of action, rather than one mass exodus that would have inevitably led to some kind of state intervention, was that the villagers should leave in small groups. Gradually over the shortest and safest period they would all become reunited in their new home of Amsterdam. William Bradford became a key player in all of this, working incessantly upon the strategies. Nothing was done without having been passed first through the Scrooby committee. Brewster's eldest son, Wrestling, had now been called permanently back to his family home and he spent much of his time with his father and Bradford. Gilbert Winslow also increased the time that he spent away from the farm giving up more and more of his precious time to be of assistance. Both Edward and Gilbert's relinquishing their homestead of many years led to greater conflict with their brothers, whom it is fair to say were still at odds about joining in. Albert's duties increased as he became a daily messenger carrying information to and fro between the villagers and the Manor. Stephen and Bill tried to keep the home on an even keel but at times even they faced a disruptive work day.

Albert had just returned back from one of his forays when he was alerted by Harriet seeking his attention in the kitchen. Bill and Stephen were not available and Liza had just informed her that the master's bed had again collapsed. Albert came to Harriet's side looking rather hot and flustered.
"What is it now Harriet?"
Harriet looked up from her pots.
"Oh, it's you, you're back then?"
Albert spoke back a little sharply.
"Yes! What do you want?"
"Are you all right, Albert? There's no need to snap, you seem a little bothered."

"Master has me here, there and everywhere, I don't know if I's coming or going. I'm sorry, I shouldn't takes it out on you, m'dear."

"'Tis all right, you takes care, it's master's bed, leg's fallen off it again and Elizabeth can't do it, can she? Please, can you?"

"I'll go straight to it while I got a minute."

So off Albert went upstairs leaving Harriet to her duties. Just at that moment Elizabeth came back into the kitchen through the back entrance, she was looking pale and drawn. Harriet looked up to see her slumping down upon the kitchen chair.

"Whatever is it Liza? First it's Albert then it's you."

"I don't know Harriet, I just been a bit sickly in the yard."

Harriet poured her some water and took it to her placing it upon the table before her.

"Here, drink this lass. It'll be something you've eaten."

"Do you think it is, Harriet? I don't know, I've had the same as Stephen and he's not been complaining. I was same t'other morning before we left cottage."

Harriet placed the palm of her hand to Liza's brow and looked at her carefully.

"You're not with child, are yer, lass?"

"Don't say that, Harriet. What with everything else at the moment it's that I was a fearing."

They continued with their discussion in the kitchen for some time before being interrupted by the two little ones rushing in. They had been making daisy chains and they were keen to show them off. Bill and Stephen joined them shortly after and Liza seemed to suddenly liven up obviously not wanting to cause concern to Stephen. Harriet then realised that she had sent Albert alone to deal with the bed and became concerned with the time that he was taking.

"I wonder what's keeping Albert?" she asked.

Bill enquired as to where he had gone and Harriet explained about the bed. Bill thought that Albert was not best suited to tackle the master's bed alone and said that he would go to help him. He was only gone a few minutes when he came back asking for Stephen. There was some amount of discussion in the hallway beyond the kitchen door and then both went away. As they began to mount the stairs Stephen asked, "But you're not certain, are yer?"

"I'm certain enough that I was frightened to speak aloud in the kitchen."

"But surely he can't be?"

"Stephen, God only knows. I hopes that I'm wrong; I just don't know what we'll do if I'm right."

"Where is he, then?"

"He's lying alongside the master's bed."

"Perhaps he's just took ill or something."

They reached the open door to the bedroom and Bill entered the room first; Stephen hung back tentatively. But then he saw for himself what he had hoped not to. Albert was lying there, motionless and grey just as Bill had said. Both men knelt down at his side and Bill raised Albert's head cradling it in both of his hands.

Stephen said, "This don't look good. This don't look good at all. Whatever was the dunderhead doing? Forgive me, Lord, Oh, my word, Albert, what have yer done? Why couldn't he have waited?"

He immediately got back up to his feet and crossed to his mistress's dresser. There lay a tiny mirror and he brought it back across to Bill. He gently held the mirror before Albert's mouth.

He examined the glass after a few moments. There was no sign of any misting. He placed the glass upon the bed; neither of them spoke a word. He then reached forward and opened one of

Albert's half-closed eyelids. There was not a flicker within his eyes.

"Oh, my God, Bill. Oh, my God, what will we do?"

Bill did not answer but continued to cradle Albert's head so gently as if it were young Damaris's. Stephen looked at him and saw the tears that nestled gently beneath the corners of his eyes. He softly removed Bill's hands from around the cold cheeks of Albert and laid Albert's head gently back to the floor. Both of the men were distraught. Stephen helped Bill to his feet.

"We have to tell Harriet," he said to Bill but it did not appear to have registered. He caught hold of Bill's sleeve and repeated, "We have to tell Harriet." Bill nodded reluctantly and then they heard footsteps behind them. Harriet walked in. She had sensed that something was awfully wrong in the way that Bill had called Stephen from the kitchen, and from the void in the time it was taking for one or the other to return. She brushed passed them and fell to the floor alongside Albert. She lifted his right hand and kissed it softly. She cupped the side of his face within her left hand, lovingly touching him, and then she began to sob incessantly, rocking to and fro. Both of the men could not speak; no words could right this wrong. No sympathy was enough.

Bill and Stephen descended the stairs together without a word passing their lips and in the hallway Liza and Natalie joined them. Bill went off to find the master whilst Stephen spoke with the ladies. He discovered the Squire sitting in the study with both of the Pastors, William Bradford and Edward Winslow. He stood gripping the door with his right hand apologising for his disturbing them.

"I'm sorry to disturb you sir but…"

The words stuck in his throat and a tear ran down his face. The Squire, immediately recognising Bill's distress, stood to his feet.

"Whatever's the matter, Bill?"

He walked to Bill's side and put a hand on his shoulder.

"Come now, surely it's not that bad?"

"Oh, but it is, sir, it's truly awful, it's Albert sir."

"Albert, what is it with Albert, Bill?"

All the others had stood to join them at the door and they immediately sensed from Bill's behaviour that it was bad news.

"We believe he's dead, sir."

"Dead! My God! where?"

"In your chambers, sir."

"But how; are you certain?"

"Yes, sir, me and Stephen found him."

The entire group immediately began to ascend the staircase when the Squire asked Bill, "Where's Harriet? Oh, my Lord, Harriet. She'll be devastated."

"She's at his side, sir. She's broken hearted."

When they entered into the room Natalie was knelt behind her father with his head resting gently in her lap. Harriet was sitting upon the master's chair alongside the bed with Liza knelt before her trying to console her. Stephen was not there, but at first the others did not even notice his absence. Pastor Smyth of the Gainsborough congregation knelt alongside Natalie and put his hand to Albert's chest and then he placed his fingers to the side of Albert's throat. He turned to the others and shook his head. Pastor Clyfton immediately began to recite the Lord's Prayer and the others joined in. Just then Stephen re-entered the room accompanied by Marion Huggins whom he had been fortunate enough to find walking in the lane.

Marion went to sit with Natalie and comforted her, then slowly she began to withdraw Natalie's supporting lap from her father's head.

"Go to yer mother, girl, she needs yer now more than ever."

Natalie stood and wiped the tears from across her face and then she joined her mother and Liza. The Squire and both of the Pastors went to them. The other men looked on helplessly as Marion began to attend to Albert; firstly straightening then tidying his limbs. She held her fingers to his half open eyes and drew them shut holding firmly on until they rested in their place. Natalie and Liza supported Harriet as she was lifted up from her chair and they guided her outwards towards the door and the landing. The Squire requested that Bill fetch one of his clean bed covers from the wardrobe and this was duly wrapped around Albert. He was then lifted and taken to one of the empty rear bedrooms and placed upon a long oak chest. They descended the stairs together only to find that Harriet had had to take a seat upon the third step as she was unable to continue. Natalie was trying to coax her mother up again, but she could not gather her strength. The master immediately sent for some of his strong brandy, from the study, for her to take medicinally. William Bradford did this and Liza offered it to her lips and she sipped reluctantly. Mary Brewster, who had been looking for her husband, was now confronted with the scene, and grasping the seriousness of the situation, whatever it might be, spoke quietly to her husband. She too was terribly shocked, but she assisted Liza and Natalie in raising Harriet back to her feet, and insisted that the ladies should all retire to the sitting room. She ushered her husband away and told him that he should look after the gentlemen. This he did, and he too insisted that both Bill and Stephen must join them in the study; then he offered brandies around to the stunned group.

Pastor Clyfton thought that it was his duty to remind the Squire that now they were without the church they were also without the church graveyard. This had occurred to neither of the others within the group, but it was true that access to the graveyard had now been denied to them. Brewster had obviously been devastated by the loss of a truly faithful friend and industrious servant and had no other thought upon his mind at this time. However, he saw that Clyfton's words were accurate and he did not hesitate for one moment in suggesting that Albert should be laid to rest in the grounds of the Manor's own family chapel.

"If we can't use the churchyard, and I fear that it is true we cannot, then Harriet's mind should be at ease knowing that Albert will be laid to rest amongst the family in the grounds that have also become their home too."

Mary Brewster had comforted the women, but because of Liza's concerns she had meanwhile made sure that the children were safe under the watchful eye of Love and that all was well; at this point they knew nothing of what had occurred.

It was exactly seven days later at 11.00 a.m. on a damp, dreary morning that Albert's family, friends and, indeed, a vast amount of the local Puritans numbering thirty or so, stood at Albert's graveside. Each and every one of them picked up a handful of the damp cloddy soil and tossed it down upon the oak casket. They then began to cross over the sodden grass and return through the orchard and into the Manor. Liza and Natalie were on either side of Harriet and never left her side throughout. In the dining room a funeral feast had been laid on in Albert's honour, meticulously prepared by Liza, Marion and Mary Brewster, whom since the day of Albert's death had been a constant rock to Harriet and the others. She helped in the kitchen whenever she could and so alleviated Harriet of some of her duties. Every one of the mourners personally expressed their love and condolences to Harriet and Natalie as they began later to leave the funeral wake. It was with the final departures that Harriet immediately took to her feet and began to clear the tables. Mary insisted that she should leave them but she would not. She said that her mourning was done. She needed to return to some kind of normality, and it did not matter how much Liza and Natalie pleaded with her, she did not listen. They helped her to carry items to and fro and she threw off her topcoat, rolled up her sleeves and began to pump water into the sink. She then began to scrub upon the crocks that the other ladies placed within whilst she quietly hummed a hymn to herself. The women reluctantly accepted Harriet's choice and recognised her need to begin her new life.

* * *

Bill, Stephen, Liza and Natalie all sat around the kitchen table discussing their fond memories of Albert with Harriet. She was now one half of a broken set, the other half, of course, being irreplaceable. Her life had reached its golden summit and now had started upon its rapid descent. Memories washed over her like rain upon glass. Her face was drawn and her mind in a continuous torture. She listened to all that was being said but the words jumbled and scattered in the violent wind that blew across her thoughts. She began to speak.

"I can never leave him now."

The buzz of remembrance skidded to a halt; all were taken aback by Harriet's sudden decisiveness. It was difficult enough to find the words to say to a recently widowed woman but Liza replied, "He'll always be with you Harriet wherever you are."

"No! I could never leave him now." Harriet was adamant.

Natalie clasped her mother's hand tightly within her own; it was as if their minds were engaged upon the same process of thought. A small tear trickled down her face.

"We don't have to leave him, Ma."

Briefly no one spoke another word. Suddenly Liza said, "You were right, Harriet, I am expecting."

Harriet's face twinged with a glimmer of emotion, the smallest of changes and the first that had been witnessed since she knelt at her husband's side. She put her free hand to Liza's cheek as she had done to Albert's on that fateful day and said, "God bless you, Liza, God bless you."

Over the next few weeks plans for departure progressed but Harriet and Natalie were no longer a party to these. No matter how hard the powers of persuasion became Harriet was firm, even the children tried because they definitely had no desire to leave their only grandma figure behind. Harriet would not budge and Natalie stood firmly with her mother. There was never a single day passed by, whatever the weather, that Harriet did not take a single flower from the garden to place upon Albert's grave. It was usually at around 11.00 a.m. and she would stand there with her head bowed for five-minutes before returning to her duties. The Squire and his wife believed that it would have been disrespectful to discuss the matter of the move too early after the funeral, so they left it for a respectful period before they met Harriet and Natalie. They were both informally invited to the sitting room to take refreshments and at this time they tried, for the last time with their own power of persuasion to influence their decision. They had to conclude that they should accept once and for all that Harriet's mind was set. There were days when Liza and Harriet sat together at the kitchen table unable to speak a word, but just sat there with tears upon their faces. Liza and Stephen's own decision suddenly returned back upon the agenda; the inner turmoil tore deep within their souls causing them to question their own desires. Stephen constantly found himself reassuring Liza that they were making the right decision, and that if Albert had still been alive then she knew that Harriet would be going too. He had to remind her that there would no longer be any future for them there and that they had the children's future to consider more than anything else. Liza knew that Stephen was right. Stephen, throughout all of this period, never once tried to influence Harriet in her decision, his heart would not let him, but he did talk to Natalie and he did ask her to try to get her mother to change her mind. He found it difficult to accept that this would never happen.

William Brewster and John Carver departed from their community for four weeks, prior to them setting a date for the first villagers' movements, in order to travel to Amsterdam and set up what was to become the beginnings of their new home and way of life. They returned to Scrooby full of enthusiasm and wishing to share this with everyone. William Bradford's news for them was that whilst they had been away the list of those wishing to travel had grown even larger increasing from what was sixty to eighty-five. This list now included the majority of Scrooby residents but also several others from the surrounding villages. The names of William Brewster, his wife, and their two sons topped it. It seemed that God had called for both of the Pastors, Clyfton and Smyth, to travel also. There was also a close associate of Smyth's who wished to accompany them; his name was John Robinson. He lived in a neighbouring village and was a former graduate of Cambridge University. The list also included the Hopkins family, Gilbert Winslow, Edward Winslow and his wife Elizabeth, John Carver and his wife Katherine, John Alden (whose family at present had no wish to accompany him but he had been given their blessings), Bill Latham and William Bradford himself. The list also included a family of tinkers that had been regular visitors to Scrooby for many years and were known by all. They were liked and accepted within the village and had been fortunate enough to be resident at the time of these occurrences. Their family name was unknown, but the village knew the father of the group as 'Thomas Tinker'. Brewster had no hesitation in accepting that they be included. This had been their longest period of residence within Scrooby now, stretching out just over five weeks.

It came to the time when Brewster and Carver realised that they could not delay any longer. Both had settled their business with their London solicitors and were more than happy with the arrangements that had been agreed in Holland. So now they decided that the exodus should begin. Carver and his wife had both been living with the Brewster's for a period having moved into the Manor house; this had allowed him to make several reconnaissance trips between Scrooby and the north coast in order to arrange passage. As agreed, this had been arranged to take place over a period of weeks in order to avoid alerting the authorities. The careful planning that had been carried out by the Scrooby committee was about to be tested. Carver and Brewster had committed the finance to the plan along with contributions by some of their more privileged sponsors. After several debates it had been decided that Brewster, Carver, Pastor Smyth and his friend Robinson should be first to go in order to ensure that everything went to plan and because they wished to take the initial risk. William Bradford, Pastor Clyfton and the Winslows had agreed that they would remain in Scrooby to ensure that the plan was a success from there and they would be the last to depart.

It was early autumn that the move began and slowly, but surely, a few at a time, the Scrooby separatists escaped from England. Their crossing to Holland over the North Sea was made in several vessels of both Dutch and English origin, (depending upon wherever the passage could be secured), and then they travelled to the city of Amsterdam. Liza and Stephen's final sad farewell to Harriet and Natalie was heart-wrenching but they were not left entirely on their own, they still had the company of some of their old friends as the Huggins's also stayed put along with the remaining Winslows. The Squire had made it, as certain as was humanly possible, that any of those reliant upon his goodwill had been ensured security after his departure, so the Broad's stayed on at the Manor. When the Hopkins family rode down the lane upon their cart with the trusty Bella in the shafts they were loaded up with their few possessions and accompanied by five members of the Allerton family and William Mullins, his wife, their son and daughter and Thomas Rogers and his family. That completed their group of travelling companions.

* * *

From the very beginning they were all warmly welcomed in their new home, but as time passed some became unsettled. It was not Scrooby. Instead, it was a strange place, with unfamiliar surroundings and the people spoke a different language. Many of the Scrooby group were uneducated and had not mastered English. They became more dependent upon others to constantly advise them. Some had left behind their loved ones and friends. Liza missed Harriet and Marion Huggins, and now that she was well into her third pregnancy she began to consider how she might cope in labour without her friend being there to hold her hand. Stephen constantly reassured her that all would go well and that there were others amongst their friends who were just as capable. They were still all as strong as ever as a family of God and William Brewster and John Carver were pillars of support for all of them. The Squire had lost his previous authority and therefore supremacy, although he was now accepted more easily as an elder of the church. Richard Clyfton and John Smyth gradually discovered that there were many distractions in Amsterdam and they began slowly to become less available to their flock.

By the time the following spring had arrived Carver, who had previously made several European connections, was making suggestions to the group that they should all move on to the nearby walled city of Leiden. He had been able to determine through his contacts that there were better opportunities in Leiden. If they were going to continue in their religious development and also as a community then the move was essential. As usual the entire group was consulted and it was made completely clear by Brewster that it had to be a majority decision before any actions could be taken. The majority did agree, with only a few declining, but they offered their own blessings for the others to continue without them. The most vocal opposition, it must be said, came from Pastor Clyfton who was totally opposed to any further disruptions in his life. He had made new associates within the ancient church and was being accepted (he was later to be ordained as a teacher there). John Smyth also chose to remain in Amsterdam having now established his own group of followers, whereas his friend John Robinson had become more acceptable to the group and he moved on to Leiden. Brewster again organised the move, ably assisted by William Bradford, who had now become fully established, always there at his side. At this time Bradford had met up with Dorothy May Bennet and their relationship had developed sufficiently that they were betrothed and awaiting their marriage.

Chapter Eight

'Leiden'

John Robinson, now adopted as the official minister for this group of pilgrims, petitioned the Leiden City Council asking them for the rights of residence there. This was answered with a short letter that read:

'No honest persons are refused free and liberal entry to the City...as long as they behave honestly and obey the laws and ordinances...under these conditions the applicants' arrival here would be pleasing and welcome.'

The names of just over one hundred people appeared upon the petition. Some of these names were not part of the original Scrooby group, as by now others had arrived from various parts of England and they had all come together joining this group in their desire for freedom and religious security.

This new move was nowhere near as arduous as the first one because there had been really no time to set firm roots in Amsterdam. In fact, most seemed to immediately appreciate their new home. There was a very good feel to this city and almost everyone agreed that the prospects seemed better in Leiden. The move for Stephen and Liza, whilst it had happened so swiftly and come as somewhat of a shock for them and the others, proved to be satisfactory, even in Liza's position. She was now caring for their new baby boy who had been born in Amsterdam. Yes, even without Marion's loving attention her baby had arrived and there were many helping and generous hands at the time. They had named him Giles. This made them now, as a family of five, the second largest family after the Allertons within their community. The christening of Giles was an urgent priority since they had left Amsterdam.

Before the main party had travelled to Leiden, as they had done previously, they had sent out a small group to prepare for their arrival. William Brewster, John Carver, John Robinson and William Bradford had all travelled together in order to establish new places of residence. A large property with land had been purchased. This was near to 'Pieterskirk' (St Peter's Church) and known at that time as 'Groene Poort' (Green Close). They were better organised now than they had been previously, and had every intention of building sufficient properties to become more comfortable and settled. They became well known within the business community and began to possess some financial influence. Brewster and Carver used this to the community's full advantage. John Robinson developed his own reputation within the local churches in order to represent his group. Temporary accommodation, lodgings and smaller local property had all been sought and secured around this area, enough for their purposes. Brewster was a gentleman and a man of honour who kept his own people very close to his heart and this meant especially the Carvers, the Hopkins's, Bill Latham and William Bradford.

Many people accepted William Bradford had become like an adopted third son to Brewster; since the final months at Scrooby they had been almost inseparable. He, having now discovered his new love, Dorothy May, meant that there was a wedding expected sometime in the not too distant future. They could not wait for their big day, and Brewster, who would act as surrogate father, was quickly trying to formulate the arrangements with them. But first, they tried to establish themselves within the new city. At this time Leiden had become well known as a city of refugees. It had two castles, 'The Gravensteen', stood at its centre and dominated Leiden; this was the residency of the 'Count of Holland' and the other, and the oldest of the two, stood upon a hill overlooking Leiden and was known as the 'The Round Burcht'. The main City Hall was very conveniently positioned local to their new residencies and so proved ideal for the purpose of a community hall. This is what they had been missing and now it allowed for them to gather together again in community and worship.

The University building, 'Academiegebauw', was very well known at that time for the high quality of the theological debates that took place there. It did not take much time for John Robinson to establish himself there and he became associated with Simon Episcopilus, a man who was deeply immersed in the Arminius teachings. Robinson also gave equal amounts of his time to his own congregation working tirelessly within the group. He wanted desperately to establish this new home for them and to gain the respect of his peers. He was not a man adverse to rolling up his sleeves and joining in with any kind of work, including labouring if it advanced their status. When, in earnest, the community began the building works of their new homes, he worked with them. They undertook to build as many cottages of their own design in the space of land that encompassed Groen Poort. Bill Latham, Stephen and William Bradford, amongst others, all laboured daily on the construction works. They had established the fact that it would be possible to build as many as twenty-one small cottages around the existing main building and they commenced with the laying down of all the foundation works. They worked for long hours at a fast pace with even the women and some of the older children helping, fetching and carrying, and supplying refreshments.

Liza and Dorothy May assisted William and his wife Mary with the construction of their new home, but the relationship between the two was never good. Any other relationship to Liza compared with that of her dear friend Harriet was a poor substitute. Liza still found that there were times when she yearned, deep within her heart, to be back at the Manor, just to be alongside the kitchen sink elbow deep in washing-up with Harriet at her side. Liza though, by now, had come to accept that this would never happen. When they were in the kitchen of the new community building in Leiden, Liza worked alongside Mary and Dorothy whilst her new baby slept in the old crib in the corner just as the two before him had done in Scrooby. Liza soon realised that neither of these women had the same watchful eye as Harriet and so, she herself had to be constantly aware of the child. Dorothy was just twenty years of age and had very little experience of younger children; she seemed to have little or no time for them. Times had changed for the Brewsters. Mary, along with her husband, had gracefully adopted her more hands on role to show her respect for, and involvement, as a congregation member. She was not uncaring, she had raised two lads of her own, but she was finding it difficult to cope with her additional work. It was obvious though that Mary was responsible and tireless in her attitude towards the education of the community's children. She was responsible for regular daily sessions within her own sitting room. These were open to all who made the effort in order that they either continue with, or commence upon their education; this was essential to the Puritans. This gave opportunities to the mothers of the group to either assist her or be available for other duties. No one was encouraged to be too idle. Whilst the children were with Mary the families were assured of their safety. Love, who was aptly named, definitely had the right attributes for working with children and he ably assisted his mother whilst Wrestling, the elder of the Brewster's boys, always worked alongside his father and William Bradford.

On the one occasion Liza and Dorothy were busy in their preparation of the lunch for seven adults and fourteen children. Not everyone had a cooked meal. Most of the men-folk working upon construction would just take bread and cheese and would often stay at their tasks. Liza was as usual finding it difficult to strike up a conversation with Dorothy, who was so quiet and occasionally moody. Liza usually found it necessary to have to introduce some topic or another that she felt may be of interest.

"How are the plans for the wedding going, Dorothy?"

Dorothly replied rather meekly, "We should have confirmation of the date by this weekend."

"That's good, isn't it? How are you feeling about it?"

"Fine." She was a woman of few words.

"Are yer not excited, lass? He's a good man, is William."

"Yes, I know but I just want it over without a fuss."

"It's a little difficult not to have fuss when you belong to a communal family such as ours is."

"I've told William I want to keep it simple and quiet."

A silence fell briefly and then unusually for Dorothy she struck up a new conversation.

"How about your young un's christening?"

"Oh, me and Stephen we said that we'd wait another month or so, besides we's aware of you and it don't seem right."

Silence descended once more. Then Liza said, "They're doing really well with the new cottages, aren't they?"

"Yes, William says that they are."

"What will you do?"

"How d'yer mean?"

"Will you get one of yer own after marriage?"

"No! William and I will stay with the Brewster's. How about you?"

"Stephen says that we're getting the first one, right next to the big house, because of the children."

"That is good, isn't it?"

"Oh, yes, I'm sure it is but it'll never replace the smithy."

Now they busied themselves about the kitchen for a while before eventually meeting back together at the huge kitchen sink.

"Has William spoken to yer about after the buildings get finished?"

"How d'yer mean?"

"You know, what will he find to do?"

"Oh, he doesn't really know yet but he is interested in the weaving, he's spoken to some of the others about it too. He says that there is a big need fer people."

"That's good. Stephen hasn't really said much at all. I probably need to give him a push because he won't be wanting to be left behind and building won't last forever."

Thomas Rogers had managed to fix his own family up with a tidy little house in the vicinity of the churchyard. He had found a new friend just across the way from them, called 'Brewer'. Thomas Brewer the head of the family was a very kind man and had immediately helped to welcome his new neighbours. He took great delight in the fact that both of them had the same first name. Rogers had no concerns in introducing Brewer to other leading members of his group. He took him firstly to meet William Brewster and in turn all of the other elders. He was not at first aware that Brewer was indeed a man of great wealth having been very astute within the financing community. Rogers kindness towards him, and, in fact, the warmth shown to him from the Puritans, led him to spend a vast amount of time with them. He was a regularly invited guest at the Brewster's household and eventually became a worthy financial and legal advisor on matters to Brewster, Carver, Bradford and Robinson. Carver was still having to travel regularly back to England in order to pursue his contracts with Edward Sandys and others in London. This meant that he was aware of the situation there and also had first hand knowledge of Holland offered by Brewer. Carver, upon his return from England, generally brought back news with him of both the political and religious state of the country. From one of his most recent trips he had returned with grave news that the King was now seeking extradition of their own group and others. This caused immediate unrest amongst them and started up discussions as to whether or not such proceedings were legal and the possibility of their success. Thomas Brewer became even more invaluable to the pilgrims. He took it upon himself to discuss the matter with many of his Dutch associates, and having raised the matter widely, when the English Ambassador approached the officials of Leiden, they totally refused to cooperate.

It was still reasonable to say that day-to-day conditions for the pilgrims in Leiden were extremely difficult. Like all other refugees, and there were many of them here, they still did their utmost to survive from day to day. Their financial resources were dwindling fast and therefore it became even more important that as the building works diminished, that wage-earning jobs should become a priority. Those who were needed to complete the building works were kept busy and those who could be spared sought to find employment. Anyone who had professional abilities did every deal that they possibly could in order to boost the community's funds. Opposite to where they were situated the Town Hall (Stadhuis) stood and just opposite that lay the tripe market (Penshal). It was here that the pilgrims went daily in search of the best but cheapest cuts of meat that they could afford. It was a rare occasion that they could afford to shop in the main meat market of Leiden. Any free land space available to them was planted out by the women and tended daily in order that they could grow some fresh produce. They were never able to achieve this in sufficient quantities for their needs.

In the March of 1610, just after his twentieth birthday, William Bradford married his betrothed Dorothy May Bennet by means of a Civil Ceremony at the Town Hall. His adopted father, William Brewster, stood at his side and in the small gathering of attendants sat: John Carver and his wife Katherine, Mary Brewster and their elder son Wrestling, Stephen and Liza Hopkins, John Robinson, Bill Latham, Thomas Brewer and his wife, Edward and Elizabeth Winslow and William and Alice Mullins. Following the ceremony they all returned to the Brewster's home where a small celebration was held. It was at this point that the children of the party joined the rest of the guests and a few others who had worked on the preparation of the wedding feast. Later in the month of April, there was a slightly larger gathering for Stephen and Liza at the baptism of their son Giles, but upon this occasion the feast was less bountiful. Brewster did not forget his usual present to the boy, passing on his coins as he had done for the girls before him.

The next celebration to be held by their community was in honour of the final completion of the building works; a topping out ceremony followed the twenty-first cottage. Slowly over a period of time their little community had been drawn back together from whence they had temporarily lodged. Once more they became neighbours at Green Close. The last completed cottage was of a significant importance to the Hopkins family, who had until now been reasonably situated, albeit in one room, of the Brewster's household. For this occasion the Brewster's home became an open house. Their kitchen was laid out with as much food and drink as they could sensibly afford but this was added to by the goodwill of any of the others with independent means. This was a time of celebration for the Puritans; they had reached a milestone. It had been extremely hard work since they had first ventured away from their humble country lives, but now in this great Dutch city they had finally achieved an important goal. This also meant, however, that the final few had reached a point where they needed to consider their vocational position. The pool of finance had, until now, supported some, although they were fully aware that this would not continue on endlessly. Some of the artisans amongst them were confident that the city had constant need for those of their considerable abilities, but the others needed to follow the many who were by now gainfully employed in the mills and factories at grinding and weaving.

William Bradford became engaged as a serge weaver in their nearest woollen mill, gradually becoming very adept at it and gaining admiration for his skill. At this time Leiden was one of the world's largest manufacturers of clothing and these were being transported all around Europe. Leiden's wool and worsted clothing was of extremely good quality. Bradford's wife Dorothy was still engaged by William Brewster, as were Liza, Stephen and Bill. Mary and Wrestling Brewster continued now to teach the younger children of the community and also became accepted childcare for their fully employed parents. Stephen and Bill set out the gardens around the cottages and to the rear of Brewster's main house; every available space functioned as allotments, with main crops of herbs, fruit and vegetables. Water was drawn from their own well situated in the close or alternatively drawn from the River Rijn. The Winslow brothers, who until now had been kept extremely well occupied with the building works, became reinstated into their old farming profession and travelled daily by cart to the extremities of the city. Edward had, having been working so closely with him for a period of time, become a very close confidante of Brewster's, and a very strong bond had grown between them just as there had with Bradford. Brewster, the better educated of the two men, bestowed upon Edward all of his worldly knowledge and Edward proved to be an extremely good student. Before his move he was a man of limited knowledge but he had developed immensely and was now a man of stature, sound education, and a source of good quality advice to others.

* * *

Five years hence had seen the group become extremely well established within the city of Leiden. They were known and well liked by many. They practised their religious beliefs without offence and offered others outside their community valuable advice whenever it was sought. During these years many more refugees from England had arrived in Leiden, coming from such places as East Anglia, London, Kent and the West Country. They all delivered news of the worsening religious conditions at home and many of them had fled leaving other family members behind them. Some had been imprisoned for their beliefs. Their spiritual leader, the Pastor John Robinson, had become well known within the churches of Leiden and had also become an established member of the Leiden University. Having been a staff member at Cambridge University, he was well suited to the position: a man of devotion possessing a quick mind being very adept in a debate. He had the ability to debate on equal terms with any of Leiden's theological supreme. Some literary works had been made unavailable, with some having been outlawed and it was a growing fear of Brewster's that a good education along with the truth was being denied to the English throngs. He discussed this matter with Robinson and many of his other close confidantes and he longed in some way to strike back at authority. He was fully aware of the risks that he was taking in holding such opinions but it became a great passion. He possessed a strong Christian faith and there lay within him a sound love of his fellow mankind. As elder to the church now, and with Pastor Robinson being engaged at times in other matters, he was now becoming more of an acting Pastor to the group.

By now Constance Hopkins was ten years of age, her sister, Damaris, eight and Giles was five. It was fair to say that Liza and Stephen had become very content with their new situation. They had a tiny, but pleasant enough cottage, situated within a loving community. Stephen still had his very good friends Bill Latham, William Mullins and Gilbert Winslow and Liza had her daily work with many companions. So now as they sat comfortably in front of their little fire late one evening Liza asked, "Do yer think much of home now, Stephen?"

"This is 'home', Ma."

"You know what I mean, d'yer think much of our little smithy?"

"T'aint no use living in the past Liza, we got our new beginning here."

"D'yer ever find yerself thinking much of Albert, Stephen?"

"Cause I thinks of Albert, he were a friend and a very good man."

"I do hope that Harriet and Natalie are faring well."

"I think we'd a heard if they weren't, Ma, after all we get enough messages coming back, don't we?"

"How long now has it been since Mr Carver last brought word, Stephen?"

"Oh, that's easy, three years since, Ma."

"D'yer think the children are happy?"

"What our lot? Cause they're happy. Why, don't you think so?"

"No, well, I don't know. I was just wondering."

"They're the most contented kids here and they got a better life than me and you ever had at their ages."

"Have you heard our Constance speaking in that Dutch way?"

"How d'yer mean, using their words?"

"Yes, course I do."

"No, I aint heard that. Tell her she needs to speak in good English like her Ma and Pa does."

"Don't be silly, they can't help but pick it up. They're gonna have different ways being over here."

"I don't want no differing ways here Ma. Mrs Brewster teaches them all well and they don't need no more learning."

Liza quickly changed the conversation.

"Dorothy's lost a second now, yer know."

"She's not, has she, lass?"

"Yes, she has. Only yesterday she miscarried again."

"That's really bad news Ma; William don't say anything, but I do know how much he loves kids and how much he wants one of his own."

"She's so moody yer know Stephen. I don't know what sort of mother she'd make but she's got little patience and gets on her high horse too often."

"Yes, I know, you always say Ma, but now she's got something to make her moody."

"Who's that girl I've seen Master Wrestling with Stephen?"

"Oh, you means Miss Tilley. He's been escorting her a while now."

"She looks like a nice girl."

"Young John's a big lad now Ma. I saw him t'other day."

"John Alden?"

"Yes, he was with the Mullins's. He's only about fourteen but he's a strapping lad."

* * *

It was now early 1617 and William Brewster had devised an ingenious plan to set up his own publishing company. Backed financially and supported by Thomas Brewer, and along with Edward Winslow and William Bradford he decided to set about publishing informative literature. The English authorities now forbade it but he still intended to distribute this as widely as he possibly could. Through John Carver he was able to reach many outlets in England which would still take the pirate publications. The publishing company was to be known as 'Pilgrim's Press'. Brewster still bore much ill feeling from having been driven from his family home, undoubtedly all down to the persecution that had been placed upon the Puritans and this was his way to strike back. He believed that the commoner was being deprived of English heritage, history and personal choice. This was a very risky business that might outrage many. The source of this clandestine press could well become known and neither he nor the others had any idea of how secure they might be. He was aware that Leiden had once stood firmly by them to deny their extradition, but this was a rapidly changing society. Besides any original writings it was decided that they must also produce reprints, and various members of the group were more than willing to contribute. Both John Robinson and Edward Winslow showed great enthusiasm for it.

So they began in earnest. It was less than twelve months before they began to receive visits from the Dutch authorities advising them of their precarious state. The English Ambassador had begun to make representations to Holland seeking the suppression of the press. The Dutch were not compelled to act but they had their concerns and so they gave fair warning. Brewster, who was strongly persuaded by Brewer and Edward Winslow's support for him, decided to continue. Thomas

Brewer's own writings expressed a strong religious belief and opinion and were in defiance of the English authorities. Mary Brewster became extremely disturbed about William's defiance and advised him of the risks that he was taking. She had always respected William for his sound judgement, but now she urged him to reconsider. She was, however, a very dutiful wife who always offered support and, respecting William's determination, she stood by him. These were very trying times in Holland and the Dutch were extremely nervous about their neighbours. They were approaching the end of a twelve-year truce with Spain and because of this they had no intentions of creating additional foes. The pilgrims became extremely vulnerable once previous support diminished.

The situation developed and during the next twelve months an ever-increasing unrest developed and spread throughout the pilgrim community. Firstly, the elders and parents were becoming less tolerant of the Dutch traits that their youngsters continued to bring home daily. Secondly, financial difficulties for them brought a strain upon their very existences. At this time Leiden's wealth began to face a general decline. Previously, the elders had seemed oblivious to the moral and religious beliefs and daily actions of the Dutch; perhaps they had been too wrapped up in their very own clique. Now they started to believe that there was an increasing threat to their form of spiritualism. Representations to William became even more frequent as the Dutch began to pressure him over the illegal printing works. Finally, following his non-compliance, both he and Thomas Brewer were arrested. Unbelievably, William Brewster later found himself being released whilst Brewer was taken across to England to be tried. Brewer urged William not to test his own good fortune by raising his voice too loudly in protest, and he gave his blessing to William wishing him well. The Pilgrim Press was immediately dismantled and the disillusionment that stemmed from these events began to fester within their community; matters were now no longer as they had believed them to be.

Following the debates of the Synod of Dort in 1619, a religious unrest grew within the City of Leiden and every religion found that it was now facing opposition and challenge. General unrest, due to the distrusting nature of the others, which had not seemed to exist before, now was prevalent upon the streets. People out walking or just trying to pursue their business began to be attacked. The pilgrims began to fear for the safety of their children. This was brought closer to them when one of their members, James Chilton, was stoned by a group of men whilst out walking with his daughter Mary. James was knocked unconscious by this vicious and unprovoked attack and had to be taken into St Catherine's Hospital. Mary had been fortunate to receive only minimal injury in the fracas and was able to accompany her father to hospital. Whilst she sat anxiously awaiting news of her father's condition she was unexpectedly approached by a gentleman. Still being in shock she did not immediately realise who the man was, but she suddenly identified him as an old friend and visitor to Scrooby; it was 'Miles Standish'. She was pleasantly surprised and happy to recognise a face at this moment of anguish. Miles, a military man, had been promoted to the rank of Captain since they had last met. He explained to her that he was making a social visit to the hospital, having spent a period of time in there following one of his earlier army campaigns. His treatment had been excellent and he had always vowed to the staff that he would return at a future date to express his thanks. He was more interested to learn how she had received the blows to her face and arm that she was now nursing. She brushed those enquiries to one side explaining them to be of little concern or relevance. Her real concerns were for her injured father. Upon hearing this, Miles immediately went off to make enquiries as to his condition and whereabouts, and came back to report that her father was comfortable, but was to be detained over night. So he offered to accompany her safely home himself. She accepted and as they walked he explained that he had been recently married to a lady by the name of 'Rose'. At present they were on their honeymoon as he had offered to show her some of the sights of Europe to which he had previously travelled. She had not wished to visit the hospital with him and he had left her at their lodgings. Mary told him of the pilgrim's adventures to date and, as he was in quite a rush now, she insisted that he should visit Groen Close the following day and re-acquaint himself with some of his old friends.

* * *

Miles and Rose sat at the dining table of William Brewster along with the Brewster family, the Chiltons, the Carvers and John Robinson. They were all busily highlighting the events of the last eleven years of their lives in Holland for their guests. He and Rose in return tried to bring them up to date with the more recent occurrences back home in England. They were also interested to learn of the exploits of his own military campaigns and he was eager to relate them. There was no lack of conversation and a general buzz of excitement filled the room that welcomed a long lost friend. It was the more recent events of the pilgrims' own experiences that Miles and Rose took a keener interest in, having been totally unaware of the present feelings of hatred within the city. For the Puritans, life in Leiden had now turned full cycle. The feelings they had when they had begun there, whilst building their new homes, had now diminished. They now seemed to be lurching from one uncertainty to another. The question that none had wished to ask, was there any long term future here in Holland for them?

After dinner the men discussed the things that had been occurring recently and their changing attitudes towards their surroundings. Brewster asked Miles about his immediate plans and how he envisaged the future for him and his new wife. Miles explained to them that he and Rose were just travelling around at the moment enjoying some leisure time. As for the future they had not yet made plans. He had been tied up for so long following regimental instructions that he now wished for his life to be less regimented.

William asked, "Would you like to stay here with us for a few days?"

Miles immediately discussed this kind offer with Rose and although Rose was a little hesitant he had no hesitation in accepting.

"That would be very kind of you, if you are certain. It would be nice to catch up with a few of my old acquaintances."

It was a pity that Miles and his new wife had arrived with such poor timing. Recently the pilgrims had become increasingly unsettled in these surroundings and many were disgruntled, to say the least.

Indeed there was now a rapidly changing heart amongst the pilgrims. It was fair to say that some had not foreseen this coming at all. Had Leiden, or indeed Holland, ever held for them what they had so much desired for in England? Religious freedom after the recent events looked a far distant dream. Did they have the independency here, where they could choose the lifestyle they desired? It was harder for the women to grasp why their men-folk had now become so disillusioned and pessimistic about the whole thing. Perhaps they had not held the same high hopes and illusions of a paradise upon earth? Everything had shifted it seemed, from calm and satisfaction, to the more extreme feeling of disgruntlement and disillusion. Miles's arrival had been the only recently good occurrence. It seemed that many were pleased to see him; perhaps because he was a welcome link to somewhere outside of their small circle? But as he became freshly associated with shadows from his past, it seemed that most questions were asked about life outside of Holland and he was pleased to answer them. This awakened in all of them a sleeping desire to return to their roots and they began to yearn once more for England. Strangely enough, though, Miles had little if anything decent to say of their homeland. Things had not changed for the better, if anything they might even be slightly worse than when they had left. It was definite, he said, that any oppression there had been was still there today. Prisons, he said, were filled to overflowing and all sorts of terrible punishments had been inflicted upon those who dared to raise their concerns. Then there was no turning back, everyone realised that but they just knew that they had not found their Utopia, and some decided that their search might lie elsewhere. The question now on everyone's lips was; where do we go from here?

Old councils were revived and people found that they were once again being asked to state their thoughts and desires. As before William Bradford found himself as a designated analyst. At the request of the elders he started to compile thoughts and deliberations upon the present situation and seek alternatives. For or against questions were asked. John Robinson, who was well established by now in the City, asked for calm and reason, he requested that everyone should think about what might be the result of hasty actions. He wanted them to look to the future in Leiden. He honestly believed that this recent unrest had just been a passing phase and that it would all blow over soon. He reminded many of them of the special relationships that they now had created in Leiden and the many and various friends they had gained from the different communities. All of this was true, of course, but they were a family and families stuck together in their decisions. So far, most of them agreed that they had reached this point together and if the majority wanted something new then they would again stand as one. John Carver was once again despatched off to England. His destination: London, in order to refresh his relationship with Sir Edwin Sandys. The word 'America' was once again being formed upon everyone's lips. America had been discussed before and most remembered the talk then of a new life, New World and new beginnings. But America would be a step into the unknown: a frightening leap into the dark for some. They had only ever received the vaguest of information about the first settlers and that had been far from good news as some of the doubters were so ready to remind them. Safety was the concern of many, but the adventure of such an enterprise aroused others. On the aspect of safety who better to consult than a man who had just served for King and Country, a man of vast experience and worldly knowledge: Miles Standish.

Miles Standish had just arrived within their midst. He was a man of very good health, being fit it seemed in both body and mind. He spoke and acted as a true gentleman and he was trusted by the highest of the pilgrims. He had already been consulted with and they appreciated his opinions, in fact, he had been heartily welcomed into their bosoms. Miles it appeared had no real plans for his or his wife's own future. He was newly married, an adventurer and a born optimist. He and his wife felt well at home with their newly made associates; what's more, he truly believed that he was appreciated and valued. The trust that they now began to heap upon him made him feel a sense of humility and honour and in this he thrived. He needed to revitalise his sense of purpose having just left the regular routine that the forces gave to him. He discussed his plans with Rose. He wanted so much to stay with the pilgrims whatever they chose to do, and he wanted to help them to establish their new lives. Rose, it was fair to say, was not awe-inspired or truly impressed. She had no desire to challenge her new husband but, unlike his recent experiences, she had found herself labouring in the kitchen at the Brewster's whilst her husband had circulated and consulted. She did not know these people as he did. She had not been an old friend, who had previously been warmly accepted into their little English village, but they had shown her no ill feeling and they had opened their houses to them both, so she reciprocated his desire.

Carver returned from England with news of opportunities. He quenched their thirst. This was all that they had needed. There were indeed sponsors willing to finance those who wanted to establish fresh colonies in the Americas. This was an untapped resource and could be the bearer of unknown treasures. Every sponsor therefore, had his price and his own interest at heart. The sponsors would trade off assistance for materialistic returns. Investors looked for others to take the risks whilst they hoped for profit. But surely this was an unmissable opportunity, as well as being financed by others. Carver talked about a land of milk and honey where everything was in excess. Brewster, Bradford, Latham, Carver, Hopkins and the Winslows all were flushed with enthusiasm. This was a chance to travel around the world, a world that was as yet untamed by others. There would be no religious interventions or other external influence or interference. Food and water for the taking in a land that could be owned and developed, with presumably untapped forests bearing sufficient timber to build bigger and better houses, houses that they themselves would possess. If all or most of this was true, then what were they waiting for?

Now William Bradford had a new list, one that grew and grew. This list was much larger than the previous one that he had compiled when they planned to leave Scrooby. In fact, he now had 400 names upon the list. These were all of people who were more than willing to join the party should the opportunity arise. Refugees from all over who had settled in Leiden now sought favour with the Puritans. Many had recently become unsettled by the troubled times in Leiden and looked for a new way out. In Holland they had failed to secure Civil autonomy and of late it looked like this would never occur. There were still many who tried to act with an air of caution and Liza's old saying 'that the grass is always greener' was often used, especially amongst the ladies. Many had concerns that this was being treated too much like a great adventure instead of an even greater risk. All of this could still end up in rather tragic circumstances. Many of the original Scrooby settlers listened intensely to the arguments of caution. They had already taken one great risk, should they take another? New names were added daily to the list but some days also saw the removal of names too. Many had changes of heart and some were placed upon the list only to be removed and later to be added in again. Some left it as long as they possibly could before having to make a final decision. It was already common knowledge that not everyone who wished to go would have the opportunity to do so. It was agreed by the elders that there would be opportunities in the future for those who preferred to follow on later, to do so. Those who had created good jobs for themselves in Leiden and were contented with their lot now had to suffer in the knowledge that those people whom they held most dear could depart and leave them behind for good. They suggested that it might be better to ride out the present storm and see what the future brought, but now that the seed had been sown and set root it could not be deterred in its strenuous growth. William Bradford had first-hand knowledge of how the decision was splitting families because his wife Dorothy May was no exception. She challenged him daily as she did not want to see the thing through to its conclusion.

In London Sir Edwin Sandys was using his good offices to try to secure for John Carver the best of the financial opportunities that had been placed before them. At the moment he had now shown a greater favour for that of the proposals put to him by a prominent London iron merchant, Mr Thomas Weston. The pilgrims' battle for survival in Leiden had cost them dearly and without sufficient backing they would have been unable to secure passage from their own meagre resources. Weston, for his part, was willing to provide the initial financing for a limited number to travel and the contract then would call upon the Puritans to honour their own side of the bargain by returning to him in due course sufficient goods to the benefit of his recompense plus a small profit. Bradford's list had grown far too long and this required the council to take drastic decisions as to who would travel and who would not.

There were names that immediately topped the list, such names that should they have not been there, would have rendered the whole episode inoperable. After that it was up to these few to decide who would constitute the full list. William Brewster consulted with his closest allies and Standish influenced him in many ways. He was concerned that an adventure of this kind into the virtual unknown, after all they had only heard snippets of information about the previous settlers, should be undertaken mainly by the fittest and healthiest amongst them. He believed that if this advanced party were successful then any others could ultimately join them. They were aware of the possibility of there being local natives wherever they arrived, and no one knew the way in which these people may react. Robinson, who still appeared to be rather sceptical concerning the whole matter, understood the general reasoning of Standish's proposals, but he was also concerned that families could be split, with some left waiting there in Holland for who knew how long without receiving information about their loved ones. Until they had definite details of numbers, having considered the available finance and the possibility of chartering a ship sufficient in size to carry them, then they could only work from provisional figures.

Finally, they did reach this point of time and it was decided that around one hundred of them could initially travel. John Robinson took the view that he should remain with those unfortunate enough not to be included. Although he was the Pastor of the group, he recommended that Brewster, the elder, should stand in place and become their new minister abroad. No one actually knew if Robinson's choice was made because of the empathy he shared with those who would not travel or if it was due to the fact that he was now a well-known and well liked citizen of Leiden. Brewster had, after all, made all of this possible. From the offset he was the prime mover, their father figure, so there were no qualms at all about him taking over their religious leadership. Robinson supported Brewster not only because of his standing but because he also had a vast religious knowledge. When the people had their say, they elected him their new Pastor unanimously. There was some conflict in the group because Miles Standish and his wife Rose had been included upon the final listing and some saw them still as outsiders who had only been with them for a short period; after all, some were leaving their own family members behind due to this. The council of elders immediately quelled this discontent by appointing Standish as their prime security advisor. He was a man of proven ability and they requested that even before they travelled he should begin to gather around him a delegation of men whose responsibility it would be to protect the others. No one could argue that Standish did not have the relevant credentials and this move was supported. Dorothy May remained silent throughout all of this and it seemed that deep within her, she still had some hope that at this point they might take their leave of the group. She was not able to fully conceal the dismay that she felt when Miles jumped at this opportunity.

* * *

On July 22nd 1620, the pilgrims boarded the '*Speedwell'*, a sixty-ton ship in the Port of Delftshaven, so as to make sail for Southampton, England. It was a sad day in Leiden for those who were left behind by friends or family and for those who were leaving them. It was the intention that the now overloaded *Speedwell*, upon docking in Southampton, should transfer a proportion of its passengers, luggage and provisions over to a second ship, thus lightening its load, and that both ships should then set sail for America. The second ship, it was said, was waiting for them in the dock at Southampton, so there should be only minor delays. On the day of sailing the *Speedwell* actually carried 101 pilgrim passengers from Holland to England, 31 of whom were children. When they arrived in Southampton there were delays; it appeared that even after all of Carver and Sandys' preparations that everything was not ready for an immediate departure. The second ship was there in dock but the cargo that was due to be loaded before the *Speedwell* arrived had not been completed and, worse still, the Captain of the second ship was still trying to procure a ship's crew. Brewster and Carver had several meetings with their financiers in Southampton. Both of them being required to sign formal contracts that they should not fail in fulfilling their part of the bargain. The financier expected that the ships would return to England with cargoes of fish, furs and lumber.

Finally, all was set for them to depart. The second ship, 'the *Mayflower*', having been made ready. It was August 5th 1620 when they waved their farewells to the Port of Southampton. It was not long however, before they found that they were forced to detour to Dartmouth, due to the *Speedwell* having sprung a leak. It took two further weeks, whilst repairs were carried out to the ship, before they were once again ready. Had they not been such strictly religious Puritans then they may well have feared that God had turned against them. They once more believed that they were waving a final farewell to England forever as they sailed away leaving Dartmouth to disappear into the mists. Tempers therefore, were very fraught when again the *Speedwell* signalled the *Mayflower* its distress and both ships again set course back into Southampton. The leaks, it seemed, were indeed worse than before.

It was a distressing forty-two days hence before the *Mayflower* finally left Plymouth, this time alone, having given up on the sea worthiness of the *Speedwell*. This meant that they were terribly overloaded, up to the hilt, as everything had been crammed aboard from the second ship. It was extremely uncomfortable from the offset and would obviously become more so as they journeyed on. The Captain of the *Mayflower* was Christopher Jones and he had with him a crew consisting of 34 men, and the total number on board was 136. The ship was equipped with masts for all occasions and it also had on board a thirty-foot launch loaded especially for the purpose of reconnaissance whenever they should spot land. Headroom below decks made it impossible for the average-sized adult to move about unless they continually stooped. Passengers had to share the storage holds in order to locate a place to sleep and there was little, if any, living space resulting in passengers seeking refuge out upon the decks. Conditions below decks were very cramped and undignified for everyone. There was a foul air which was sickly and nauseating and if it hadn't have been for necessity no one given a choice would ever have chosen willingly to stay there.

Chapter Nine

'The *Mayflower*'

Mayflower **Passenger List**
John Alden
Isaac Allerton, Mary Allerton(wife), Bartholemew Allerton (son)   Mary Allerton (daughter). Remember Allerton (daughter) Don Allerton (no relation)
Don Billington, Eleanor Billington (wife)
Frances Billington (relation unknown), John Billington (son),
William Bradford, Dorothy May Bradford (wife)
William Brewster, Mary Brewster (wife),
Love Brewster (son), Wrestling Brewster (son)
Richard Britteridge
Peter Brown
William Butten
Robert Cartier
John Carver, Katherine Carver (wife)
James Chilton, Susanna Chilton (wife)
Mary Chilton (unknown relation)
Richard Clarke
Francis Cook, John Cook (son)
Humility Cooper
John Crackston , John Crackston (son)
Edward Doty

Francis Eaton, Sarah Eaton (wife), Samuel Eaton (son)
---------Ely (sailor)
Thomas English
Moses Fletcher
Edward Fuller, Ann Fuller (wife) Samuel Fuller (son)
Samuel Fuller (physician not related)
Richard Gardiner
John Goodman
William Holbeck
John Hooke
Stephen Hopkins, Elizabeth Hopkins, Giles Hopkins (son)
Constance Hopkins, (daughter), Damaris Hopkins (daughter)
John Howland
John Langmore
William Latham
Edward Leister
Edmund Margeson
Christopher Martin
Desire Minter
Elinor More
Jasper More
Richard More
Mary More
William Mullins, Alice Mullins (wife), Joseph Mullins (son)
Priscilla Mullins (daughter)
Degory Priest
Solomon Prower
John Rigdale
Alice Rigdale
Thomas Rogers, Joseph Rogers (son)
Henry Sampson
George Soule
Miles Standish, Rose Standish (wife)
Elias Story

Edward Thompson
Edward Tilley, Agnes Tilley (wife), Elizabeth Tilley (daughter)
John Tilley, Joan Tilley (wife)
Thomas Tinker, Wife of Thomas and Son of Thomas (unknown)
William Trevore
John Turner, 2 Sons of John (unknown)
Master Richard Warren
William White, Susana White (wife), Peregrine White (son), Resolved White (son)
Roger Wilder
Thomas Williams
Edward Winslow, Elizabeth Winslow (wife)
Gilbert Winslow (brother).

Liza Hopkins was six-months pregnant and she was the only pregnant woman on board the *Mayflower*. It is fair to say that she had more than a large share of female support on board. Stephen was very concerned for her well-being and indeed that of the unborn child. Being on board an ocean-going ship was not the best place to be with child. He had, even if it had been a little light-heartedly, suggested that they should stay in Leiden. However, Liza knew Stephen better than that and she would have none of it. Constance, Damaris and Giles, like every other child on the ship, loved every minute of it. It was a great adventure for all of them. Children of their ages had none of the adult worries to concern them. Mary Brewster continued to educate the children and had to follow a daily routine, but prevailing weather conditions did not always allow for this. Dorothy May Bradford was morose and she definitely found her soul mate in Rose Standish. Dorothy had neither the passion nor the driving ambition of her husband, whereas Rose dreamt daily of other places and things that she would rather have been doing than to have been stuck there aboard the *Mayflower*. The crew took care of the ship, thus leaving the men with plenty of time to plan and scheme their future existence.

A twenty-year-old John Alden found time to consider his future, his life possibly, on his own. Since he had left his family many years before at home in Scrooby, there was a chance that he would spend his life alone. It is fair to say that he did only consider the future, he certainly did not dwell in the past, and now he believed that he saw his future clearly. Priscilla Mullins was the prettiest girl aboard. She had golden curly hair, pale blue eyes and a ruddy complexion. Her eyes sparkled with life; she had good manners and was also one of the best-educated ladies there. Within days of their setting sail, John had his eyes and mind focused firmly upon one thing. Whatever it took, he had to win her affection; she was the girl for him. He became a very determined young man. He confided his thoughts to just one man: the man who from the moment they had been introduced began to be his mentor. Miles Standish promised that he would help in whatever way that he could. He promised to initiate some sort of approach for him. He would guide him and encourage his ambitions. John had competition from both Resolved White and John Crackston, but Miles reassured him that Priscilla had eyes for only one person and that was John Alden. Unfortunately, John was naturally shy and found it difficult to do things for himself, but Miles pursued his cause diligently and at every opportunity the wooing took place. Miles Standish was so persistent in this that at times it was rumoured that he pursued the girl for himself.

Constance Hopkins was now fifteen years of age and she too was maturing into a delightful young lady. She had long hair that fell to the middle of her back. It was a mass of brown curly ringlets and her mother used to love to sit behind her and brush it out with a fine bone handled brush that had been given to her by

Mary Brewster. On this particular day she was doing just that. It had been a pleasantly warm autumn day. They had spent a long day on deck away from the miseries below, but there came a time when it was safer to be there than up top. Her other siblings were throwing wooden rings, trying to place them on wooden pegs. As children that age are wont to do Damaris, Constance and Giles were continually asking their mother the same question.

"When should we get there, Mother?"

"Oh, you keep asking me that same question over and over Constance. We'll get there when we get there. It won't make it come any quicker, you keep asking all the time."

"Does anyone know just how long it takes or is no one sure?"

Damaris who had been concentrating upon the hoops, said, "I asked Ely the sailor who joined us at Plymouth, and he said that he's sailed there afore and he reckons it takes seven or eight weeks generally."

Liza replied, "Yes, and we all know what tall stories Ely tells."

"Will we be there for Christmas, Ma?" asked Constance.

"'Course we'll be there then, lass and long afore I hopes. I'll be there for the new baby to be born, you'll see."

"How long have we got to wait now fer the new baby, Ma?"

"Two to Three months, lass. That's what I say, we'll be there."

Upon deck, now that the women and children had retired, Miles was putting some of the young men through their paces. He had been asked by William Brewster to prepare a fighting force and that was his intention. They were well aware that they could be repelled as soon as they attempted to go ashore. At present there were about twenty of them using varying lengths of timber as makeshift staffs and they were sparring rigorously with one another. He was also trying to help some of them to build up their rather puny bodies. For this purpose he had had them running, jumping and lifting heavy objects. Some of them were also acquainted with the use of swords and firearms; so there were times when he had straw men tied to the masts for them to practise upon. They also used these same targets whenever they used bows and arrows, but Brewster restricted this to certain times to avoid any nasty accidents occurring. Miles knew his work; he was a true artisan and the men had already begun to sharpen their ability within the short period that they had. In Plymouth a man called William Trevore had joined the ship's party; he was a Cornish man and excellent with both the sword and the bow. He too, like Miles had fought in many campaigns. Brewster had accepted his request to join the pilgrims after having discovered this fact. But more importantly, Trevore was experienced in both sailing and sail making and was known in Plymouth to be generally useful with small boats and fishing. Brewster recognised this as a real asset amongst so many country folk.

Besides everything else below decks, they also had to keep their livestock. They had sufficient for a start in the New World with chickens, ducks, geese, pigs, goats and hares. Gilbert Winslow was placed in charge of looking after the livestock and Thomas Tinker and his family assisted him. They also were never short of additional volunteering children. Carrying livestock meant that they had the problems of carrying sufficient feed, dealing with their waste and putting up with the smells that they emitted. They had no intentions whatsoever of slaughtering any of these animals during, or indeed for quite a while after, the voyage. These animals were an investment for the future. The present benefits were a few eggs and a small quantity of milk, none of which was sufficient for the needs of their everyday menu. It did supply a minimal source of fresh produce though and Winslow distributed it to those whom he believed were in most need. Food on a voyage of this nature had a degree of uncertainty about it. How much food do you store on the ship to ensure there is sufficient for the journey's length, if the time it will take is uncertain? Another difficulty was how to prepare food for a hundred or so people aboard a ship that had little, if any, facilities for the voyagers? When the preparation and cooking of the food took place most of the womenfolk gathered together to play their part; food was heated in small coal pans placed upon sand boxes and sheltered from the wind. The risk of a fire occurring during cooking was a real enough danger for them all to be instructed to take the utmost care; fire aboard a wooden ship out at sea was the last thing that any of them wanted.

Captain Jones was a weathered seaman who appeared to know his work well and fortunately he had selected a crew who were good honest sailors. If Brewster ever felt the need to approach the Captain with a matter of concern it was always dealt with most efficiently. One matter that they could not improve upon the *Mayflower* was the living conditions; these were appalling. It was no use complaining although some, in particular Dorothy May, did so anyway. Most of the others cooperated as one family and tried to make the best of worsening conditions. Captain Jones, ever the gentleman, was aware that he had a woman aboard whom was big with child and he enquired of her condition daily. He also made the effort to try to see her as often as he could to reassure her that everything was being done to arrive at their destination without delay. Liza did not want to contemplate the alternative, but Brewster assured her that there was a good physician on board and so many of a helping disposition that she need not fear for lack of the right attention. Liza needed to reassure Stephen more about her needs. She told him of how courteous the Captain was and of the attention that all of those around them were showing. Stephen, however, had a greater concern for the child after its birth than before it was born. This was no place for a baby to either be born or to start its life – the smells below decks where Liza would be confined were putrid.

The delays that had been caused by the *Speedwell's* condition at the commencement of the voyage had been extremely irritating for everyone; the consequences of this had meant that temporary lodgings for those ashore needed to be found. But for the even more unfortunate, this had meant that they had already spent this period of delay on the *Mayflower* and they had needed to feed themselves for that time too. Their finances having been drained to the lowest point ever, meant that the shortage of rations aboard the ship was of great concern. Some of the individuals' own resources had been strained and they were too proud to admit this. The depression of that entire episode had only lifted as the distance between England and the *Mayflower* expanded daily. There had been moments during all of that madness when some had feared that a journey back to Leiden was a greater possibility. After the first week at sea a routine had developed. Passengers slowly developed their space; they had regular meals and most importantly for them they had regular religious services. So now it was only those who had a general discontent about sailing, concerns for the future, or resentment at having been drawn into this in the first place, who continued to grumble. Dorothy May and Rose Standish, to a lesser extent, were prime examples of the latter.

William Brewster, with even the best of advisors, found that it was extremely difficult to plan for the unknown. Even with their almost daily counsels and with everyone's best intentions there was still an amount of uncertainty. Ideally they would have preferred to be undertaking such a journey at a different time of the year, but circumstances beyond their control had been the final judge of this. The length of the journey relied even more upon the prevailing conditions that might be expected during this autumn to winter period. If, when they arrived, they found that the reports arriving from the first settlers had been true, then they expected that the land, which greeted them, would be vast, wild and rugged. If this was the case, then William's plans were that an immediate community shelter would need to be constructed and so they needed to be prepared for this possibility. They expected to find huge forest areas, so finding enough timber should be no problem for them. If they were fortunate enough there may even be quantities of rock that would also be helpful. With this type of surroundings in mind, they also believed that there must be sufficient wildlife for hunting and capture. Wild horses, apparently, ran free around the countryside. The local native population might prove problematical, as they may not take too kindly to a large number of people suddenly descending upon them and stealing their resources. They needed the natives to understand their needs. For their part, they meant no one any harm and would do their utmost to live amongst the indigenous people peacefully. It was, therefore, understood that Miles Standish's role was to be that of a protectorate and there was to be no offensive taken against the native population. They intended not to deprive others of what was rightly theirs, and were to immediately offer to live as friends.

Standish had no problem with what was expected of him or with the men that he was training. He hoped, in fact, that he had seen the last of the unnecessary fighting and disharmony brought upon others. His past army campaigns would be sufficient enough to see him through his life. If any sort of confrontation occurred then he had agreed that this would be discussed with

Brewster and the other elders. He had just as important a role in the reconnaissance of the shores that lay before them. They would quickly need to establish that wherever they intended to disembark had sufficient resources, with the most important commodity, being water. They planned to build the community shelter to house them all as a means of becoming established whilst the *Mayflower* was filled with the produce to honour their contract and sent home. If the first priorities were achieved then the rest should follow on. With all of this in mind, they organised lumberjacks, a construction team, a hunting and fishing team, and teams for labouring and housekeeping. Any of the older children would help, whilst Mary Brewster and some of the other ladies kept the younger children safe, educated and out of harm's way and, of course, Standish aimed to defend them. Forward planning was that after the individual shelters had been established the initial community hall should act as the church hall and be used for social gatherings.

Whilst Miles was preoccupied with all of this planning, his wife Rose was left to her own devices. This was not how she had envisaged her life following their recent marriage. At one moment she had been enjoying her European tour and suddenly a whirlwind of activity, new companions and a frenzied activity filled her life. Rose had from the offset been aware of the unhappiness of Dorothy May and she tried to be a good companion to her. They were two different characters. Rose loved her husband and although she would not have chosen this path for herself she saw how much it meant to Miles and she too liked these people. Dorothy May did not like it. Rose saw that she grew ever more morose by the day. Rose tried to help others and she became involved in whatever might need to be done. She had very little spare time in her days. Dorothy May did only what was expected of her. She did not socialise or converse with others. She spent far too long below decks in the putrid atmosphere and no matter how Rose tried to coax her to take regular daily strolls, she seldom had success. Instead of taking an interest in her husband's work, she was indifferent to it and tried to discourage him. There seemed to be a jealousy that existed between them. Too often when she saw that he was engrossed with others or the centre of attraction she would stride off in a bad temper and sulk in some corner. William really loved her but she was blind to this. He tried to console her but she was indifferent to his efforts. Whenever she saw him with any other female she would become unnecessarily outraged. He encouraged her daily, as did Rose, to become more involved with things around her, but she closed her shell tightly. There was monotony at sea; everywhere looked the same and the scenery did not change. The sun rose in one position and sank in the other. There were salt water and fishy smells above, and urine and body odours below. Everything lingered for day upon end. Dorothy May needed help but she refused it. Small children tried to befriend her, she just rebuked them.

Some days, with a good wind at their backs, they made excellent progress, but there were others, sometimes for days upon end, when the lull caused them to drift about aimlessly. There were days when the gentle stroking breeze failed even to billow the sail canvas and left the flags hanging lifelessly. For three such days now the *Mayflower* had lain in becalmed waters and the frustrated grew ever more so. Then on the fourth day, a balmy wind struck up and the sails were teased into life. The water lapped upon the stern's dark timbers and rippled away beyond. A casual but gentle momentum developed gracefully apace and drove the *Mayflower* onwards. Objects began to roll about and some fell from the tops of casks, crates and tables. William Brewster and John Carver, with concern, went forward to consult the ship's captain. Everywhere crew members sprang into life adjusting ropes and sails and beckoning for the passengers to make haste below. Captain Jones was confronted whilst checking their path and issuing instructions for realignment. The increasing pace and the onward propulsion was like a new course of blood within his very veins and this is what he had waited for. Brewster spoke with a questioning uncertainty:

"This is looking better, Captain?"

"Yes, but you never know how long it might last, as you've seen the calm can hit yer just as soon."

Carver seeming concerned said, "Its intensity seems to grow by the minute."

The Captain just replied, "'Tis no concern, let's just see where it has the will to take us."

Brewster enquired, "Do we know with any more certainty of our position, Captain?"

"Let's just say we're turned half-way and if this continues to blow we'll be making up fer lost time."

"We're concerned about the food reserves – have we allowed for enough to sustain us?" Brewster asked.

"Who can truly say but we'll have our good and we'll have our bad days, we'll make speed whenever possible. No one can account fer the wind, but no one need fret as yet sir."

"Good, Captain, we'll take our leave and let the others know. It might boost dwindling spirits."

The calm that had greeted them that morning was no longer present throughout the day, because as it progressed the wind increased in strength. Doors that had been either tied or pegged open, in order to release the stale air from below, now had to be latched. The sails snatched at their bindings and shook furiously. By the time that early evening had arrived, the onrush of the *Mayflower* threw the waves up across the decks washing them on its way. In comparison to the previous lengthy lull, this sudden stride had the effect of lifting the heart and mood of those on board. People talked excitedly, ate and drank more, and busily tidied their restricted living spaces oblivious of the stench. It was later that night that some eventually began to show their real concerns. This newfound wind strength, at first seen as the blessing that they had all been praying for, now had developed to such an extent that they feared for what might happen. It certainly was the fiercest of conditions yet faced upon this voyage. Those below listened intensely at the rattling and banging above. They also listened, as they heard crew members come and go above their heads, at the mumblings of alarm. Some of the loose items from on deck had to be hurriedly rushed below causing even more cramped conditions and ropes were called for from anyone who had them in order to lash things down.

That night those who had been fortunate enough to get off to sleep had still been frequently awakened by the sudden jolts, lifts, drops and bangs. A child's voice was heard to cry out and sometimes more than one cried in unison. Screaming voices above were distinguished at times above the howling and whistling wind. Before dawn finally broke, the sky was lit intermittently with chains of lightning and thunderclaps so loud they appeared to vibrate the timbers. Besides the usual stench there was now a lingering smell of vomit. Since setting sail for their first time some had experienced seasickness caused by the constant motion. Many who until now had managed not to, now submitted to the constant stir. Most of the young children suffered from this, as now did the majority of adults. The *Mayflower* had been brutally tossed like a man astride a bronco with the incessant roll of the waves. It was a scene of inexpressible suffering amongst the bales, the barrels and between the restrictive head beams. Winslow and the Tinkers had, at times, needed to lie across, or physically hold down some of their livestock. Parents also did this with the children, as they feared for the way their offspring were being hurled about. Vessels used in haste to contain liquids and excrement had been slung into corners and left drained. Stephen was more concerned than ever for Liza in her condition; both fought for their children but Liza suffered for it. Stephen had fetched the physician, Samuel Fuller, to her side. Constance sat moistening her mother's head and lips with a dampened cloth; she had been a great strength to her parents in this crisis and Damaris also tried to help. Stephen hung on tightly to them, trying to calm his weeping son. He repeatedly mouthed reassurances but they, unfortunately, fell upon deaf ears.

By 10.00 a.m. it was agreed that the hatches must be opened briefly so that the men and some of the eldest youths could clear away the night's spoils. It was still raining heavily and as the contents of containers were thrown over board lashings of waste were splashed back aboard swilling around amongst their feet. The Captain sent a message to William and the elders to go to him urgently and they did. He had been witness to such conditions many times before, so therefore he stressed that attention must be given to cleaning up their conditions on board because there was a real risk of disease. Miles organised a working party and for the next few hours everything below was scrubbed and mopped. This task was doubly difficult because, although the ship had settled considerably since the night storm, it was still far from calm and some passengers were still suffering from the conditions. By 2.00 p.m. that afternoon the storms had once again increased in ferocity. This meant that even if they had the appetite to eat, and most didn't, many hadn't eaten since the night before. It was in fact impossible to set up their small sand boxes on deck. Liza's condition had improved for a while during the lull and then deteriorated again later. The physician had advised that she must stay horizontal, be kept calm and given as much water as she could take. Stephen was very concerned but acted bravely to ensure that the children did not fear for their mother. He did exactly as the physician had instructed and continually reassured Liza that the storm would not last for long and that all would be well. The physician was finding himself more occupied with other passengers. The biggest problem that most faced was losing so much body fluid which led to dehydration. An elderly lady had now become his biggest concern. He was satisfied that Liza was in capable hands and that they would fetch him if required. Mary Chilton was looking very ill; her health had not been good anyway and now these violent occurrences had been too much for her.

Mary had suffered for a while from bouts of dizziness and the unstable conditions only added to her misery. To add to her problems she also had an ulcerated leg, caused originally by a knock she had received when boarding the *Speedwell*, that had meant she had not been able to get upon deck too often and therefore was exposed to the worst of the conditions for much of the time. The physician had been administering painkilling drugs for the past two weeks. Mary by now had become pale and incoherent. James and Susanna, who were relatives of hers, grew very concerned for her. James fetched William Brewster to her side. William, the appointed Pastor, immediately saw how grave the situation was and began to read prayers over her. All of those around her, upon seeing this, immediately prayed too. Mary's breathing became increasingly laboured and it was difficult for her carers to attend to her now that the *Mayflower* had begun to roll around precariously again. She had to be tied down so that she could be held firmly in place. Throughout the night a constant vigil was kept. At around 4.30 a.m., the lightning was again flashing about them and the thunder appeared to be much worse than the previous night. Often utensils and other items were thrown about the place: candles, candleholders, pots, pans and shoes. Anyone attempting to move about bruised their bodies, arms and legs as they were thrown against the ship's timbers. Mary Chilton died at 6.00 p.m. on that day; no one could have done more to save her.

That following night was much the same as the two previous ones. The wind howled constantly like a pack of baying wolves. The *Mayflower* swung and turned, lurched and shook, rose and fell. Water swilled down below decks and men blindly panicked to clear it away. A chain of them passed buckets hand to hand through the ship and up the wooden steps as they bailed for all that their strength allowed. Even the more intrepid amongst them now feared for their lives. Stephen hugged Liza tightly and the three children all huddled together tightly in their own little corner. There was a constant banging above them, but none so frightening and breathtaking as the almighty cracking, roaring and crashing that occurred at around 3.00 a.m. Screams could be heard from all quarters. Everyone thought that the deck would collapse above and stifle them where they lay. Prayers were shouted out loud and could be heard even above the children who cried continually. No one could say what the cause of this latest sound had been; they were left only to guess. Brewster immediately asked that everybody should be checked to make sure of their safety. All were found to have survived whatever had occurred. Up on deck, unknown to them, catastrophe had struck. A deck beam mid-ships had split under the wind's constant pressure. It had been torn apart at its shaft just above deck level. As it had dropped it had ripped apart the one sail and unfortunately had struck one of the crewmen, Noakes, about the face and shoulder. Noakes had been knocked unconscious and his shoulder blade had been shattered.

The crew fought with the flailing sailcloth and rolled the mast from the body of Noakes. It was only when Fuller was called above that word had begun to get back that they realised what had happened. Miles Standish and William Bradford were also sent above to see if help was required. They were both confronted with the mayhem of that night. Noakes was lifted with extreme caution, as instructed by Fuller, and carried by six men across to the Captain's cabin. Here he was placed upon the tabletop. He remained unconscious throughout and rumours started amongst the crew that he was already dead. The physician attended his wounds under the watchful eye of the Captain, Bradford and Standish. All tried to help him in his attempts to save the man. The physician strapped his arm tightly across his chest, having realised the damage that Noakes had sustained. He applied spirits to the lacerations across his face and shoulder and laid a dampened cloth about his head. Noakes eventually began to regain consciousness, slowly returning from that state, he groaned loudly and seemed unaware of his position and the cause of it. It had all happened so suddenly without warning. He needed to be given strong spirit to calm him down and Miles offered to sit at his side for the rest of that night. The crew were set to lashing the main beam down to stop it from being lost overboard. By now the rent sail had been gathered in and taken below. Captain Jones went about his job and weathered the worst of the storm, containing any further damage. By morning Noakes's condition appeared to have improved, much to the surprise of many, and Fuller continued to treat him. Slowly, from early morning onwards, the storm began to lose strength and by 11.00 a.m. that day it had simply withered away sufficiently enough for passengers to be appearing up above and walking the deck.

Early that same afternoon Miles, and some of the strongest men, aided other crewmembers in hoisting the shattered beam to its former position. Ropes had been attached and drawn above to hold it secure. The ship's carpenter had prepared the shaft that had been left protruding above and the foot of the beam had been chiselled and shaved. Lashings and fixings had been prepared to try and remount it. The men struggled as the beam heaved about before it settled eventually in a position that satisfied the carpenter. Timber straps had been torn from crates and wooden dowels prepared. An auger was used to place holes strategically about the face. It was extremely difficult to work between the legs and arms of the men who supported the whole structure throughout, but the carpenter was persistent in his task. It was lashed temporarily, then the large dowel pegs were knocked home, and just to ensure its rigidity the timber straps were bound tightly around it and tarred. There it was pinned and fixed back in its previous position looking extremely precarious but appearing sound. Finally, the holding ropes were gently let away, one at a time, checking as it went. It stood there pointing to the sky. It was for certain that anything anywhere near to half as strong as the last night's storms would cause it to fall again. But for now it stood there and was a job well done. The sail was drawn from below but found to be irreparable; fortunately additional sails had been stored so this was no real problem and the cloth had many other uses. Eventually, when all was restored and the weather was holding fair, the *Mayflower* continued to make good progress. They had no worse conditions for the rest of that week, so they had time to recover.

Frederick Noakes, the injured sailor, who had at first rallied round, gradually became unwell again. Fuller grew concerned for him and advised Captain Jones. Noakes had lain incapacitated by the damage since that night, but had been able to converse and to take food and water. He had at one point asked to be raised to his feet but his legs were weak and unsteady, so he was returned to his temporary bed. The grazing and cuts had started to scab over and the bruising and swelling to his head and face was receding. He had lost the use of his arm and Fuller had told him that this would remain the same for a time to come. Visiting to see how he was, Fuller found him blacked-out again oblivious to the world about him. The Captain was called and Brewster also attended. It was a matter of minutes before Noakes became aware of things again. Over the next few days this became a regular occurrence. Each time the man seemed less aware of just who he was and appeared to be losing his faculties. He went on like this surviving seven days since the event of that night, but upon the eighth day, when one of the crew members attempted to awaken him, he could not; the physician was immediately called for. Frederick was found to be dead, having died peacefully in his sleep. Exactly ten days after Mary Chilton had been cast overboard to a watery grave and offered to her Lord, Frederick Noakes now joined her.

The following day the storms returned. Fortunately, they were nowhere near as awful as those that had preceded them, but they were bad enough. Amazingly the repaired mast stood up to the renewed pounding. A lot more sickness prevailed and much more time had to be spent cooped up than anybody would have wished for. Liza was a very hardy lady though, and she fared much better than some of the others. She did still suffer the sickness but not near as badly as she had done before. This storm blew itself out in just over twenty-four hours and this time no unfortunate consequences resulted from it. The *Mayflower* had now been at sea for five weeks and Liza's baby was due in mid-November. Captain Jones still could not predict accurately enough when they might arrive in America. The storms had delayed their progress and, he feared, blown them somewhat off-course. When Liza spoke to Stephen and the children about the new baby she never feared any problems. She was always confident that matters would be well and so she usually discussed names.

"'America', that's what we'll call the new baby, it'll be very fitting to our new home."

"Boy or girl?" asked Stephen.

"Yes, either, boy or girl, 'America Hopkins', it sounds good."

"It's definitely befitting the first baby born to the Puritans in America, that's sure enough."

The children loved it too. Constance thought on, and asked, "When will we be there, father?"

Stephen gave Liza a wry smile and replied, "Not that old chestnut again Constance. All I can say is soon enough, I'm sure. Fer now you be content in yer adventures and help yer Mom and t'others."

Over the next week the *Mayflower* rode in and out of storms all of less severity than the first, but severe enough. The Puritans grew concerned for their conditions and their rations with still no land having been sighted. Then on one of the clearest of clear, blue sky days when the *Mayflower* glided graciously upon a glassy ocean, Damaris came running to fetch her father, very excited and breathless.

"Calm down, Damaris, what is it?"

"It's me ma, father, it's me ma!"

Stephen hung tightly to Damaris's hand as she strained at his arm pulling him forward across the deck towards the hold.

Once below he could see that the physician was stooped before Liza, as was Rose Standish.

"What is it?" he asked as he hurriedly approached, "what is it?"

Rose answered him and the physician carried on about his business.

"It's the baby, Stephen, Liza's in birth."

Stephen knelt down at her side gathering her left hand into his and gripping it firmly. He then stroked back her hair from her sweating brow. She turned her eyes towards his and he saw a grimace upon her face.

"It'll be fine, Liza you'll see, it'll be just fine."

Damaris had returned to Giles and they sat upon the floor threading beads upon wool. Constance returned with water and a cloth that the physician had called for. She placed a comforting hand upon her father's shoulder when she saw that he was now there. Just then Mary Brewster arrived to help. She looked reassuringly at Stephen, whispered something to Rose and then suggested that the children went to find Love for her, as he had something he wanted to show them. Constance protested a little about having to leave, but her father nodded to her to do as she was requested. Mary moved across to the opposite side from Stephen and took up Liza's other hand.

"Everything's good Liza, have no fears."

Mary then took a moistened cloth and damped Liza down, cooling her off. She had a lavender bag in her possession and she placed it alongside Liza's head to help smother the awful smells that provided around them. For the next two hours Liza screamed as a procession of willing helpers came by offering to lend their hands. They were all advised that nothing more could be done. One person who did not attend was Dorothy May, which surprised very few people. Constance regularly returned to ask of her mother's well being but she was told that all was well and occasionally was asked to refresh the water supply.

Much to Liza's eventual relief the baby did arrive; it was a second son and he was fit and well, two or three week early, albeit. The physician and Rose Standish cut the cord, cleaned up Liza, and then Rose and Mary towelled down the baby before handing it safely to his mother's arms. Giles and the girls were sent for to welcome the new family member and were greeted by their father who still sat at Liza's side with tears occasionally rolling down his cheeks, so proud was he of his wife. Brewster and Carver were the next to arrive having been alerted that a new pilgrim had joined their family. Brewster immediately offered up a blessing for the boy. Later, as things started to quieten down, just the gloating father was sitting there, Stephen whispered softly to Liza, "It wasn't quite as we planned it, was it, lass?"

Liza gave Stephen a very tired smile and then replied, "No, but it's over now. God's blessed us with another son and we should thank him fer that."

"He's a bonny baby, Liza, it's true enough. So, this is little America, then?"

"No, Stephen, don't ask me why but I lay there thinking and I believe if it were meant to be then he would have been born there."

"But I thought we all agreed, Ma, babbies as well?"

"You know babbies, Stephen, they'll understand. I thought not America but something to do with voyage."

"But what might that be, Liza?"

"Well, he's been born on the ocean Stephen, maybe we can make something of that?"

"Yes, I know he's born on the ocean but we can't call him 'Ocean', can we?"

Liza thought for a few moments, gently caressing the baby's tiny hand.

" 'Oceanis', Stephen."

"Oceanis?" Stephen replied.

"Yes, 'Oceanis'."

She immediately called the three other children to her and said, "Meet yer new brother, 'Oceanis'."

They immediately liked the name. There was not one argument and so it was agreed. Oceanis it would be.

The joy of new life aboard the ship after the earlier losses brought great pleasure to everyone. The proud parents were bestowed with many little gifts, many of them handmade. New life had come to the *Mayflower* so even the underlying worries of where they were at sea and if they would ever see new land was pushed aside for a few joyous days. Then the Captain called for Brewster and Carver to go to visit him; for the first time he honestly seemed to be concerned about not knowing their definite whereabouts. He was mainly concerned about their continuing existence as each day brought them a colder breeze and worsening conditions, exacerbated by a shortage of food. He was definitely right about the weather as most days brought a cold, clammy mist that hung about them. His fear about rationing had been playing upon their minds for some time now. They had to organise this, but at the same time they had to make folk believe that they grew closer to their destination and that all would be well. William decided that it was advisable that he should speak to them all together and he made this arrangement. They had, the elders, made a plan of action and as long as they stood by this and kept faith then they believed that God would do the rest. They tried to ensure them that none of the women or children would go without and that the men would try to take the greater burden.

Needless to say, even the elders' assurances that all would be well, did not much convince those who had begun to tire of this journey. Fear of having insufficient food to complete the journey started the doubters talking about the possibilities that they may never arrive in America. Mothers feared mainly for their children and vowed that they would not go without whilst any food remained. Discussions regarding the livestock on board began, and it was decided that, if needs be, then they would kill these. Ely, the sailor, was a worthwhile man to have on board. Whenever things were none too well he had a way of lifting people, and he was especially good with the young ones. He recognised when things were looking dark, so now he wrote a little sea shanty especially for the pilgrims and he had the children gather around him whilst he taught it to them.

Pilgrims' Shanty

Oh come all ye puritans gather round me
For we're on a journey way over the sea
We came from a country that don't understand
So we're off together to find a new land.

Blow bonny sail; blow us on to the shore
Blow bonny sail, blow us on ever more
Deliver us on to a land that is free
Blow bonny sail, blow us over the sea.

Oh come all ye puritans sing strong and loud
We'll follow the Lord and he'll see us all proud
He'll give us a home that is better than most
And raise up the winds that'll bring us the coast.

Blow bonny sail; blow us on to the shore
Blow bonny sail, blow us on ever more
Deliver us on to a land that is free
Blow bonny sail, blow us over the sea.

Old Ely's Shanty worked wonders for the pilgrims. For days the pilgrims could not wander the ship's deck without hearing it either sung or hummed by child or adult alike. Before that week was at an end land was finally sighted. Unfortunately, none were at all certain, including the Captain and his first mate, where they exactly were. The winds and rough sea had driven them so far off course that it was hard to tell for certain. As the *Mayflower* drew closer and closer in towards it they spotted whales for the first time. The majority of them had never seen a whale before and at first they feared what might become of the ship. The date was the 11th of November 1620. They had not expected to see the mass of whiteness that lay before them as the snowflakes fluttered gently down upon them. Lying enticingly and beckoning them on in was the widest of bays. Everything was sharp on the eye with such blinding reflections from the low sun and snow-smothered land. Having been alerted to the sighting the deck was now a swarm of bodies all jostling for a better view. Even Dorothy May for once wanted to be up on deck. All hoped that this was to be their newfound home although, at first sight, it was less enticing than their anticipations had been. Some of them dropped to their knees and shouted out praise to the Lord; their daily prayers answered at last and deliverance granted. Immediately the elders asked to meet with the Captain, now was the time to start to put their long awaited plans into operation. Most of the discussion was at first about location; had they arrived at where they wanted to be? This was of no certainty at all. Having signed binding contracts back in England, they needed to ensure their legality and comply with exactly what the financiers had asked of them. Captain Jones advised them that he had more immediate concerns as to how close he could risk the *Mayflower* into shore. He ordered lookouts to the bow and soundings to be taken regularly so that the anchor should be let out at the first mate's orders. Eventually the *Mayflower* set out its anchor in the middle of the bay, close enough to be able to see the shoreline with the snowy covered outline of forests and hills in the distance.

The *Mayflower*, having been tossed upon stormy waters and hammered by raging crosswinds for a good part of the eight weeks it had taken, sat ghostly and almost motionless upon the smooth waters of the bay. On board there was an anxiety mixed with excitement, intrepidity and longing to finally set foot upon the land that beckoned to them through the mists. As everyone had spent so long below decks in the tiniest of holes and cramped quarters and having to put up with the daily stenches of vomit, urine and body odours, no one amongst them wanted to spend any longer on board than circumstance dictated. There was an immediate fervour for disembarkation. But, however anxious the pilgrims were, all the planning that had been made had not allowed for people to go rushing out into the unknown. Brewster, Carver and Standish all stressed the caution that must be taken and did not want anyone to act foolishly. They were after all, about to leave a reasonably safe environment in order to face an environment unseen before by any of them. It was already too late on this particular day for anyone to consider leaving the *Mayflower* and journeying to the shores, so it was agreed that they must wait until the new day arrived.

It was decided that another meeting should be held between all of the elders and Captain Jones and his first officers. Between them it was believed that they should get a rough bearing of their actual position. In the cabin several charts were unfurled upon the tabletop and everyone studied them intensely. One of the difficulties was that they had approached this land without having travelled the coastline, and so they were not fully aware of it in detail, which did not help. Captain Jones had in his possession the more recent chartings of Captain John Smith, the leader of the first colonists there. From these it was agreed that they had been blown well off course and were possibly not now facing land that had previously been charted by the London Company. This then would be in breach of the contact undertaken by them. After what they had all encountered over the last few weeks and now to come to this realisation was not what anyone of them wanted to hear. They were not in the mood or the physical condition to continue further. It had taken longer than any had expected and the food rations were now dangerously low, if nothing more, then they must go ashore to replenish these. The final decision taken that night was that Miles Standish should early the following morning take the landing boat and his reconnaissance group out to explore the shoreline. The Captain agreed that the thirty-foot launch would be lowered early enough by the crew and made ready for their departure. All of the group must be armed in case of confrontation, but they agreed that this should be avoided if humanly possible. Brewster insisted that no more than ten hours must be spent ashore before they would report back with their findings. He could not stress enough how important it was that these orders be complied with. The launch was by far the largest of the boats on board and he did not wish to have to send out a smaller party in search of the first.

Many of the pilgrims had very little sleep that night simply because of the excitement that filled the air. The night itself was also the coldest they had endured during the whole journey. They awoke early the following day to be confronted by heavy downfalls of snow. The *Mayflower* sat there with icicles hanging about the decks and a coating of snow. It was decided that they must delay their departure. By mid-day conditions had still not greatly improved and the majority of the passengers had spent this time huddled together to keep warm below decks. This brought further disappointment to an already flagging group. This is not how they had envisaged their arrival. Further meetings took place during that day. Brewster was concerned about the *Mayflower* and its crew being delayed, but Captain Jones assured him that he too was under orders not to return without his ship being fully loaded with saleable goods. So they did not intend to go anywhere. It was then of some urgency that they should find camp, set up and begin to do what they intended. Brewster was, however, pleased in the knowledge that the ship would be their shelter until they could provide for themselves. With time on their hands, and nothing more to do, Brewster began to write, having consulted with the elders, a document that they intended should give them legality, structure and government in their new home. It was insisted by most, although there were a few dissenting voices, that this must not be seen back home as a rebellious document, and to ensure this there was full agreement that an allegiance should be sworn to the King. Even if their enforced departure from England had left a sour taste with most, and the King was not the most revered ruler, their loyalty to England had never been in question. It was believed that total separation and isolation in such a desolate unknown land would not have been the wisest of choices.

By late that afternoon, having realised that they were in an area uncharted by the London Company, they had composed a document that received everyone's support; this was later to be known as, 'The *Mayflower* Compact'. All of the males above twenty-one were consulted and given an opportunity to contribute and all appended their signatures to the final document. It was a majoritarian statement stressing their continual allegiance and intended to be their first major contribution to a democratic government for the new settlement. Everyone there who had made a contribution believed that it would ensure a basic structure for co-operation, compliance and survival. There were forty-one signatures on the completed statement. One mystery was that the man previously known to all of the others only as 'Ely', and said to be the bearer of no other known name, had when requested to, signed with the signature of Chester Chesterson. This is what the compact stated:

'In the name of God, Amen. We whose names are underwritten, the loyal subjects of our dread soveraigne Lord King James by the grace of God, of Great Britaine, Franc, & Ireland king, defender of the faith, e&. having undertaken, for the glorie of God, and advancemente of the Christian faith and honour of our king & countrie, a voyage to plant the first colonie in the Norterne parts of Virginia, doe by these presents solemnly & mutually in the presence of God, and one another, covenant & combine our selves together into a civill body politick, for our better ordering & preservation & furtherance of the ends aforesaid; and by virtue hearof to enacte, constitute, and frame such just & equall lawes, ordinances, Acts, constitutions, & offices, from time to time, as shall be thought most meete & convenient for the generall good of the Colonie, unto which we promise all due submission and obedience. In witness wherof we have hereunder subscribed our names at Cap-Codd ye.11. of November, in the year of the raigne of our soveraigne Lord King James, of England, France, & Ireland ye eighteenth, and of Scotland the fiftie fourth. Ano: Dom. 1620.

John Carver; Digery Priest, William Brewster, Edmund Margeson, John Alden, George Soule, James Chilton, Francis Cooke, Edward Doten, Moses Fletcher, John Rigdale, Christopher Martin, William Mullins, Thomas English, John Howland, Stephen Hopkins, Edward Winslow, Gilbert Winslow, Miles Standish, Richard Bitteridge, Francis Eaton, John Tilly, John Billington, Thomas Tinker, Samuel Fuller, Richard Clark, John Allerton, Richard Warren, Edward Leister, William Bradford, Thomas Williams, Isaac Allerton, Chester Chesterson, Peter Brown, John Tuner, Edward Tilly, John Craxton, Thomas Rogers, John Goodman, Edward Fuller, Richard Gardiner, William White.

With the practicalities now appearing to have been attended to everybody on board wanted to be able to get their feet upon solid ground. The journey had been too much for many to bear. The food rationing and the storms had made the journey an unpleasant one. It had gone on longer than most had expected and they were bursting with the need to get on with life. Several had misunderstandings and believed that it would be possible to arrive in such a place and just commence from where they had left off. They needed to establish the colony and the elders fully understood the difficulties to be faced. They, perhaps, had not explained well enough to the womenfolk that it wasn't so simple a matter as to all rush ashore and set up camp. The children were especially restless having been cooped up for such a long time in such ungodly surroundings, which left them with excess energy to burn up. Brewster had to calm everyone and to explain the need for patience at such a crucial time.

Chapter Ten

The Bay of Cape Cod and Plymouth

The conditions the following day were much more favourable and so the launch was lowered and made ready to be boarded. Miles was taking with him fifteen of the fittest men aboard. He had personally trained them all and he knew just what their capabilities were, therefore he was happy that they were all fit and able. They all pulled hard on the oars as they left the side of the *Mayflower* accompanied by a cheer from some of those on board who had awakened early enough to see them off. Miles looked out from the bow of the boat towards the shore keeping a very sharp eye upon the beach for a good landing place, as well as for any sign of movement.

The mouth of the bay was very wide, bigger than they had ever seen. Miles knew from how difficult it had been for the Captain to find a safe place to set down anchor that it was very shallow in parts. Previously the *Mayflower* had needed to circle about the bay in order to find the safest and most convenient location closest to the land. This nearest point still left them about a quarter of a mile out. The water was clear beneath the launch and they were able to see many varieties of fish below them. They closed in upon a long beach with many different kinds of trees to the rear, and they saw that there were lots of craggy rocks that made it difficult for the boat to go right in. Miles decided that rather than take a risk, the boat must be left where it was. So they clambered out into freezing cold seawater that rose above their knees, and then secured the launch firmly. Some of the men immediately noticed the large shellfish about the place, which had the appearance of mussels. Once upon the shore, those who had gathered some, opened them up, to find that they were extremely fat and also contained a sea-pearl, another was tried and this too held the same. They decided that when they returned to the ship they would gather more and take them back.

Some of the men shook with cold and suffered from the dampness and Miles feared for their health if they were to be out for the rest of the day. John Alden, who had the previous day been the youngest signatory to the compact having just reached twenty-one, took off a topcoat and threw it around one of the elder men. The others who had accompanied them were: – William Bradford, Bill Latham, Richard Warren, John Crackston, William Holbeck, John Hooke, Edward and Gilbert Winslow, Francis Eaton, Ely, William Butten, Robert Cortier and Richard Bitteridge. All were ready for what they might find. Each man was alert and full of the joys of having been the first group to place their feet upon this new stretch of land. Their plan was to carry out reconnaissance of the land about them, taking note of vegetation and creatures, if, or not, there were any favourable living areas. Was there a good supply of timber and fresh running water? Miles reminded them to be ever alert, keeping an eye open always for the presence of any other living beings. If they found any recognisably edible plants then they were to take some back with them. They split up into five teams of three, each with one nominated leader, and Miles instructed them that they should only walk for a moderate distance at first and return frequently to the shore to be certain of their return. He had also decided that he had no intention of taking the full-allotted time on this their first day on new land. He wanted to ensure that nothing untoward had occurred. Some had more expertise with the vegetation and Miles had tried to organise them in such a way that their experiences complemented each other. Within only a few minutes of entering the woods he himself had accounted for oaks, pines, juniper and had found some others that were unknown to him or the others in his group. The most important thing, that he was looking for was a stream, river or a source of water, without this one factor alone it had been agreed that they should venture elsewhere.

Obviously the forest floor vegetation was not a true representation of what they might find upon the more open spaces, but every time they came towards the edge of a clump of trees, in sight of a clearing, the drifts of snow were often knee deep, in fact, the conditions were so bad that it was difficult to make out any of the underlying vegetation. Movement across these open spaces was made all the more difficult because of the depth of the snow and they had to wade through, suffering the severity of the cold. After a few hours they had witnessed, in their small groups, a variety of birds and animals, but they had not located either running or frozen water. The clearings were flat and exposed them to sharp cutting winds, not at all pleasant to be searching through. Initially, they had all moved off in a wide sweep towards the east, but having found nothing, they returned and started to trek out in a more westerly direction. It was not long into this search that one of the groups saw in the distance a group of Indians moving in their direction and decided to be very cautious as they had no idea what sort of reception they may receive. So they started to alert the other groups to the situation. There was a sudden whistling and a thud as an arrow hit a tree less than ten feet to the left of Miles. Miles immediately reacted by placing his arm defensively between him and his party and ordering them down to the ground.

"Where did that come from?" he asked.

Crackston replied, "Just behind that clump of trees there."

He pointed in the general direction. The men had already prepared their weapons but Miles ordered them not to return fire. They watched for a few moments and eventually saw two natives scamper from one hideout to the next.

No further arrows followed and after a short period of keeping low, Miles suggested that they should retreat.

"I believe it to be a warning, they don't want us here, it's obvious and I have agreed with Brewster that we'll not go where we are not wanted. Let's just fall back towards the others and move off. We can't afford to face a confrontation."

Hooke, the other member of his trio, had no hesitation in agreeing. It also appeared from continued observation that the natives were not in pursuit of them.

Miles drew them all back together slowly as they retreated towards the coastline. When they believed that they were no longer being observed, it was agreed with the rest that this tribe was generally acting in a threatening way. They explained that they had managed to keep a reasonable distance from them, although eventually they were fired upon. Miles did not see this as an intentional bodily threat upon them, but as a serious warning that they were definitely not welcome. Some of the men wanted to return and exchange fire, but he advised against it and suggested that they took their leave quietly. There would be other more welcoming places, he was certain, and he had no intentions of taking unnecessary risk.

When they returned to the *Mayflower* they did not deliver the report that all were wishing to hear. Instead they advised the elders that they would not be kindly accepted in this area. Miles though, did not hesitate in showing his enthusiasm for what little they had seen and rather than heighten the pessimistic feeling that this news had delivered, he informed them that they would return the following day, better prepared. This time they would enter the forest further towards the west where the lay of the land appeared more favourable. With regard to their unwelcoming reception, he said that they were only a small group and he hoped that they could avoid any further conflict with them. Those who had returned with the mussels that they had gathered, offered them to anyone wishing to try them. The elders were interested in the pearls that had been found inside of these; from now on they would need to be permanently vigilant for the possibilities of wealth that could ensure support from back home and, inevitably, their survival. As far as the resident natives were concerned then they had never had any intention of confronting or dispossessing others of their rightful lands. Miles suggested to the elders that it might be wise to bear gifts from the ship upon their return, and if they did meet the natives again then they could leave them somewhere for them to find, so that they might understand that they had friendly intentions. They had to adjourn at this point in the discussion, because it seemed that those who had eaten the mussels had become ill with stomach cramps and severe vomiting. Brewster reminded everyone that this was exactly what they had to be careful about. The next time there was any uncertainty as to what they had found, then someone would have to volunteer to taste and check the food before several of them suffered in this same way. There were a few hours of real concern and the physician had to render treatment, although it seemed that no long-term harm had been caused.

The next day the launch returned to a point much further along the beach with the men on board much better prepared for their adventure. Some of those men from the previous day had developed coughs and sneezes, because of the cold conditions. This day too was unfruitful. No one had confronted them but

Miles was still unhappy with what they found. Again the people who awaited them were despondent, however Miles had no fears that he would find for them the right place. Over the next few days Miles and the men started their search further and further towards the west of the bay. Those who remained daily upon the ship became more disgruntled. Many of them had believed that upon their arrival all would go ashore and begin to build their selves a new life, but this is not how it was. Each day in order to ease the concerns over the ever-dwindling food stocks the reconnaissance team hunted whilst they searched and returned with fish, meat and fur. Whilst back on the *Mayflower*, to overcome the boredom, everyone was busied with preparation for when they were allowed ashore, and, in order, to occupy the older children they were set to fishing from the deck. Daily now the table had a supply of cod and other assorted fish whilst the snow was melted down to supplement the water supply. Because the launch had needed to travel further each day, Captain Jones decided that the *Mayflower* should move along the coast; this was agreed. They finally eased away from the bay and turned the point to see a mass of land running off into the distance before them.

The ship set anchor for its final time on the 15th day of December; it had been a month since they had arrived. It was on the previous day that Miles had at last returned to the ship with the news that they had all longed to hear. He believed that he had found the right place for them. It was as he stated to the elders, more readily inhabitable, with all of the conditions that they had desired. There had been no inhabitants encountered and he honestly did believe that this was it. As the news filtered to the others at last they believed that they would set their feet down upon solid land, but this was soon denied them. Miles recommended that until a sound shelter had been established, large enough to house all of them, then it would not be sensible to leave the minimal comforts of the ship. The ground was still frozen solid and some days had been so unbearably cold that his team had suffered greatly. The better news was that daily more and more of those willing to could be taken ashore, which would hasten the construction of their new community building. William Brewster and Carver trusted to Standish's sound and sensible advice. Until now he had caused them no reason to doubt this, and all who had arrived had been kept safe and well. The elders completely supported the suggestion that work parties should go out daily, so now everyone who wished to would have his first opportunity to step upon this new home soil. This would give them new reason for hope.

The land that had been chosen by the pilgrims unfortunately was believed to be uninhabited, but this was for a very good reason. A recent plague had all but wiped out the entire population of the local tribe. The few remaining members had moved camp, constantly believing that they were leaving the disease behind them. Eventually, probably because of the freezing weather, some had survived a distance away. Of course, the pilgrims were oblivious to the risk of plague knowing nothing at this time about its previous existence, and were therefore running the risk of transferring it from land to sea every time they made their journey to and fro. If contractible the plague would, no doubt, have wiped all of them out. Such were the conditions back aboard the *Mayflower* now with such a poor diet for everyone, that so many were lacking in their vitamin requirements and many had begun to take ill with one or more disorders. A lack of fresh fruit and vegetables on board and frozen ground on land meant that they had no way of subsidising this shortage. The intense, enduring cold aboard, led to the oldest and the youngest developing colds and fevers. Samuel Fuller, the ship's physician, soon discovered himself unable to cope with the ever-increasing medical demands. He spent little, if any, time ashore as his entire days were preoccupied with treating the sick. Scurvy soon followed the fevers and this was followed by pneumonia and tuberculosis. Isolation had to be arranged as some were contagious, which proved extremely difficult aboard such a small vessel.

Liza and Stephen had tremendous fears for their children, particularly the recently born Oceanis. There were days when Stephen refused to go across to the land for fear that his children might not be looked after in the way that only he could assure. It soon became a topic for conversation that they had been brought all this distance only to die within sight of land, unable to go ashore. William Brewster and the other elders were constantly answerable to those who began to question their leadership. Remonstrations were daily occurrences and some demanded that they be allowed off the ship. A meeting was called and Miles Standish spoke on behalf of the elders. He assured everyone that whatever the conditions on board they would be at an even greater disadvantage ashore until things were made ready for them. Work upon the community hall was extremely slow; every day they were hampered by the unbearable freezing winds. The artisans working with their hands were suffering from pains in their finger joints, and the lumberjacks after struggling to fell the trees had then to transfer the trees from the forest to the building site sometimes in knee-depth snow. Most begrudgingly accepted the difficulties, but they were concerned that these grave illnesses meant that if some progress was not urgently made then they might yet all perish.

Dorothy May Bradford, the worst of the disillusioned, had by now become unbearable to many and unapproachable by her few companions, she was totally withdrawn. She and William spent all of their time arguing these days. William believed that once he could get her ashore with everyone else then things would begin to improve. The physician discussed her ailments regularly with William and he now feared that she had indeed become mentally disturbed. William was told that whenever he was not ashore he must keep a careful watch upon her, and when he was away, he hoped that Rose Standish would care for her. Dorothy, as far as Dorothy was concerned, had on this one day had a reasonably good day. William had returned to the ship to be advised by Rose that she had been a little more talkative and less argumentative. Rose said that Dorothy had even managed a smile or two. William was exuberant with the fact that matters may well be improving. After they had eaten, and most of the others had settled down for the night, Rose suggested to William that Dorothy might take a stroll up on deck. He was pleased with Rose's suggestion and, after helping Dorothy on with warmer clothes he was about to do the same but she said that as he had been out in the cold for so long that day that he need not go. Dorothy assured him that a walk on her own was exactly what she needed. He politely tried to change her mind but she said that there was no need to worry for her, as she believed that things would get better for him. He kissed Dorothy and thought he was doing the best for her in letting her go. He sat waiting for her, drumming his fingers but after thirty minutes had passed he knew that something was not as it should be. He put on his outdoor clothes and went in search of Dorothy, but she was nowhere to be seen. He asked the crew and only one of them said that he had seen her briefly toward the stern of the ship and she had wished him good evening. William continued his search and then he called in to see the Captain as no one had seen Dorothy. The Captain immediately ordered a search of the ship but Dorothy May Bradford was never seen again.

Having lost her closest confidante, Rose Standish took to writing letters to England to relieve both the stress and boredom. Most of these were written to her long-time childhood friend,

Cecile Longfellow, wife of Joseph. Of course she had not also become demented, she was well aware that until the *Mayflower* had long since left them behind, none of these letters would reach her intended recipient. She kept a daily diary, but this remained always within her possession, and she believed that this would be her way of telling her homeland of the New World. She kept the letters firmly tied together with a length of red hair ribbon until the day that they might leave her. Rose became a regular nurse assisting the physician on board the *Mayflower*. With so much serious illness, he needed the help. During this period Miles left the ship everyday because he was a constant amongst those on shore. They saw each other for such small amounts of time that she became even more possessive of him when he was there. Because he was away for such long periods and was still trying to assist Alden with his wooing, he endeavoured to continue with his matchmaking efforts on Alden's behalf, and this had raised Rose's suspicions concerning his fidelity. He insisted upon acting as a chaperone to John when he was with Priscilla and Rose resented this. Of course, Priscilla being one of the prettiest maidens on board, was attracting a great deal of male interest. However, Alden singly adored her and his constant wooing seemed to be bringing slow rewards. Misunderstanding this situation, Rose used her letters to Cecile to open her heart about Miles and Priscilla and the fears that she had of losing him to her. She did not confront Miles because she adored him and wanted nothing to threaten their relationship.

As everyone had long feared, the eldest and youngest passengers had become more prone to the suffering that had befallen the ship. This soon began to have its toll when secondly, Susana White, wife of William, died of pneumonia; within two days three children followed her dying from the scurvy. They were, Remember Allerton, Maurice Turner and Samuel Eaton. Under the conditions that they had been experiencing for four weeks or more aboard the ship and on the land there was nothing more that could have been done to avoid this. The time or conditions were still not right for them to leave the ship and over the following few weeks several more of the passengers became victims of the various illnesses and died. It sickened their hearts to be a witness to the suffering and to have no powers available to them to remedy the situation. They could not up anchor and journey back home, because they had no resources to allow for this. For them all to have left the ship with no permanent building completed upon shore, without medication and no freshly grown produce, they would still have seen the same demise. By the second week of March 1621 the *Mayflower* still lay at anchor and the surviving numbers had diminished to less than sixty. It was not until this date that the weather conditions, having improved greatly, saw Fuller the physician relieved enough to report that all of the ailments were now under sufficient control and that there was now no continuing fear for the loss of life.

Captain John Smith's chartings, having been thoroughly examined by Captain Jones and the elders, had now led some of them to believe that the land that they had chosen to settle upon was New Plymouth and the bay that they had sailed into upon first sighting it was Cape Cod. It was pure coincidence that having been blown off course, and being totally unaware of their positioning that they should have left Plymouth, England to arrive in Plymouth, America. It was March 21st when those still on board the *Mayflower* were ferried into their new home. On arrival they were greeted, with loud cheers by those already there, every time the boat arrived on shore. They were led into the newly, constructed log stockade that surrounded enough cleared land for them to see at close hand the large community building that had been constructed of rock and timber. Some other smaller buildings had already started to be raised from the ground, and those who had not been ashore before to see this were full of admiration for what had been achieved under extreme duress. Inside the large meeting hall a store of farm tools had been gathered into a small room at the rear. In another one any food remaining on board was being stacked upon shelves or hung from hooks. Bunks had been constructed along the entire length of the hall and at the one end there was an extremely large stone fireplace with an enormous log fire burning within. Everyone who arrived brought with them various pots, pans, blankets and furs that had been accumulated over the last few months. They all had their own personal belongings that no longer amounted to much, although sufficient for a new start. When everyone was gathered together in the hall and the large wooden doors closed and latched behind them, William Brewster and John Carver stood and addressed the company.

This address was the first of its kind in their new environment and developed into the first of many religious services to come. Even after the suffering and loss of that winter they praised the Lord for His goodness and for His deliverance. There had been such dark days recently when death followed death and some doubters thought that this day might never happen. John Carver made an impressive inaugural speech that lifted all of their hearts, but readied them also for still harder days to come.

> 'This is not a time for resting on one's laurels. This is a time for hard labour, a time for thanksgiving, and a time to look to the future. This is just a beginning. What we do from now, and the way in which it is done, will be the history of tomorrow. We have to set the foundations in this new and fertile land for all of our future generations.'

John Carver stood down to the sound of cheers and hoots. Immediately Brewster in support of his friend stood to his feet and without hesitation proposed that Carver be elected as the First Governor of the New Plymouth colony. There was not a voice raised in dissent and Carver was duly elected.

That night, for the first time, Liza and Stephen Hopkins slept cosily in their new bunks in the warmth of the community hall. Liza had Oceanis at her side, and Constance, Damaris and Giles all slept upon furs strewn between their parents' bunks. This was one family that was still intact after having survived the horrors of the past months and they were still fit and healthy. Miles Standish and Rose occupied one of the already completed outer cottages, as did the Brewsters and the Carvers. This was the first night in the last seven that Stephen had been at Liza's side. He, along with Standish, Bradford, Latham and many of the other men, had recently been resident working long hours upon the completion of the hall's construction. One of the other cottages, already started, would be the Hopkins's upon completion. In the meantime, the hall would serve as a home for them and the other remaining pilgrims and some of the ship's crew who had laboured alongside them until their return to England came.

In the previous few weeks, Miles Standish had reported a sighting of one or two inquisitive natives, but as of yet there had been no approach towards them or signs of unfriendliness shown. There seemed to be more interest shown in what they were doing and why. Since their arrival in this new land there was not a night past by without sentries having been posted to keep a watchful eye by both day and night and this would continue for now. Miles advised the elders that he saw no reason for them to fear the neighbours who appeared few in number anyway. Miles had always suspected that this place had had previous inhabitants, because of the cleared land areas, but he had his beliefs consolidated with the arrival of spring and the thaw. The newly exposed land revealed signs of recent cultivation and spring life was evident. The natives were becoming braver by the day and approached closer and closer, merely observing and appearing to offer no threat.

Within days of them inhabiting the settlement, the Winslows, whose task it was to prepare the land about them for sowing purposes were approached by a single native who just sat and watched their actions. After two previous visits and without any attempts at communication the same native arrived on the third day bearing gifts of beaver skin and a sack containing seed. He placed these upon the ground at a safe distance away, then he walked away but remained within sight. The Winslows collected the gifts and accepted them signalling their thanks towards him. It appeared from these encounters that he meant them only goodwill. Everyday, after that first day he had been seen, he would continue to arrive daily. He gradually became brave enough after this to help if any of the men were struggling and appeared to have need of it. He initially made no attempt to communicate, until he eventually shocked both of the brothers by speaking to them in reasonably good English. He enquired, "You are English?"

After a short hesitation, not believing what they had heard they replied, "Yes."

Edward then asked, "But how, I mean, how do you know the English language?"

His was a very interesting story and he proceeded to explain to them that he had actually been taken by force to England, but had returned since to rejoin his tribe. It appeared that he had spent a few years on a country estate in England, where he had been treated well and had been taught some English. He told them that his name was 'Squanto'.

That night the Winslows could not wait to explain to the elders the occurrences of the day, as well as the bemusement that they had felt hearing a native speak to them in their own mother tongue. Everyone was interested to meet him and to hear more of his story, but it was suggested, by the elders, that they should not approach too soon as it may appear as a threat to him. He needed to be reassured that they meant him no harm and so it was agreed that the Winslows should continue to build upon the relationship. The following day, he brought with him some stinking fish. This he smashed with rocks and scattered upon the soil where they were planting, which seemed to indicate good intentions. The Winslows being aware of many agricultural practices, saw this as being similar to the practice of manuring back home in England, to enrich the soils. Squanto was gradually introduced to more of the pilgrims who became interested in his behaviour. They all carried some small gift that they offered to him.

After a week or so had passed other natives appeared and began to watch over the pilgrims. Squanto encouraged the natives to come forward, because these people meant them no harm, but they reacted in different ways. Gradually they accepted their visitors and were accepted in return. Soon the visitors were introduced to Carver and Brewster and it appeared that they understood that these were the pilgrims' leaders. Then for a few days afterwards it was noticed that none of the natives arrived during the morning as had become normal procedure. Later that day a great procession arrived with several new faces never seen by the pilgrims before. They also brought with them their females, known as squaws, and a few children. Most impressive of all was the man who led the procession, who appeared at a distance to be elderly and highly decorated. The procession caused much excitement in the new colony with everyone dropping whatever it was that they were doing to go to witness it.

Carver and the other elders greeted the decorated elder with a firm shake of the hand, and on this occasion instead of them stopping outside of the stockade they were all led proudly in with the pilgrims' children clambering to see them. They were taken straight into the community hall where everyone else gathered around them. Squanto introduced the leader as 'Ousamequin'. They understood that he was the chief of the tribe. He held out his arms and hands palms up. Seeming to represent his acknowledgement of them. He then said several times, 'Wampanoag, Wampanoag'. Immediately Carver called for food and drink to be offered to the guests. It was very difficult to be able to express how they felt because there was insufficient understanding between the two groups. The children appeared to find it easier as they showed their small hand made toys off and demonstrated their use. Two of the braves of the tribe offered more gifts to them of blankets and seed. Ousamequin was the centre of attention. He was old but appeared strong; he had a deeply tanned complexion, and he was wearing a feathered headdress comprised entirely of yellow feathers that hung below his waist with rows of glistening beads and bangles about his chest, waist, neck and arms. The visitors stayed for about two hours and then Squanto, who by this time was more associated with the ways of the Puritans, was able to tell the Winslows that they had to leave. If he was to be understood correctly, then they had been invited to the tribe's camp on some future occasion.

The elders of the pilgrims were impressed with their guests and now had little doubt that they could live together in harmony. The 'Wampanoags', as they now understood them to be, had been cordial and friendly. The gifts they had brought, especially the seeds, suggested that this would be a good trading partnership. Brewster discussed with Carver the need to draw-up some sort of official treaty so that if they did go on this return visit, which they saw no reason not to do, then they could present this and make their relationship more binding. It was viewed as being a genuine gesture of friendship rather than as a legal document. This was agreed and Carver set about drafting the treaty for approval of the elders.

As usual Squanto was there the following day as he had been every day since he first came to see them. Indeed, he put as much time into the ploughing and sowing as any of the others did. He made Edward Winslow understand that on the following day he would lead them to the tribe's camp. Edward immediately fetched Brewster to confirm this arrangement. The elders saw no reasons whatsoever why they could not live alongside the Wampanoag, and if this first real contact with the native population had been anything to go by they should have a friendly coexistence. The treaty was made ready to be offered to the tribe but not to be pressed upon them; they intended to discuss the future of living alongside each other as friends. They realised that the main difficulty to overcome was being able to converse well enough to do this. Squanto led all of the elders, their wives and a few children to the camp. The pilgrims did not want to arrive there and completely outnumber their guests. The few children were taken because of the friendship that had been struck up two days earlier.

On arrival the pilgrims found a very small camp with no more residing there than those that had arrived at the stockade the day before. These were the only ones that had survived the plague, but at this time the pilgrims were still totally unaware of this fact. The children were sent off to play whilst the adults were invited warmly to sit with their hosts around a central campfire upon woollen fleeces. Chief Ousamequin offered around a long smoking pipe. He took one long puff upon it, then he passed it towards his right and all of the others were expected to do the same. Not wishing to offend, no one declined the offer. The Wampanoag squaws then offered food around the circle. Everything was done in as friendly a manner as on the day before and the pilgrims were made to feel extremely welcome. Ousamequin even sent for one of the smaller tribal headdresses and presented it as a gift to John Carver. After the meal Edward Winslow did his best to explain to Squanto about the treaty document by showing it to him and appending his signature and then asking Squanto to do the same. Squanto did not do this at first, but he did stoop to speak for quite a long time to the Chief. It seemed that they understood what was intended and the Chief took a few of his tribe and beckoned for Carver to join them in the largest hide wigwam. Both Brewster and Carver offered their hands to the Chief in friendship and sat with him. They showed him the treaty and placed their names upon it. Ousamequin spoke firstly to his elders and then to Squanto, who was younger than all of the others, and after a short while it appeared that they had made a decision, and they placed their names also upon the treaty. Brewster had drawn up a copy of exactly the same document. This too was signed and handed over to the Chief. Despite the language difficulties and the brief time they had been acquainted it seemed that everyone was happy with what had occurred.

The peace treaty document read: -
- That neither he (Massaoit)(Ousamequin) nor any of his people should injure or do hurt to any of our (the pilgrims) people.
- That if any of our tools were taken away, when our people were at work, he should cause them

to be restored: and if ours did any harm to any of his, we should do like to them.
- If any did unjustly war against him, we would aid him; if any did war against us, he should aid us.
- He should tell his neighbours confederates of this, that they might not wrong us.
- That when their men came to us, they should leave their bows and arrows behind them, as we should do our weapons when we came to them.

They were all happy about the outcome but the pilgrims believed that no hasty actions should be taken in enforcing the issues until they believed that they were properly understood.

Due to their diminished numbers, and having to concentrate so much of their time and effort since arriving into establishing themselves, the pilgrims had found it impossible to provide both for themselves and to sufficiently load up the *Mayflower* for the return journey. The contract that they had made was something that they so dearly wanted to comply with, but Captain Jones had for a long period now been concerned with the time it was taking before he could make the homeward journey. Sadly, it was agreed that the *Mayflower* should be let go, free to sail. They had done their best and still intended to do more. John Carver agreed with the Captain that it was unfair to both him and his crew to be stranded in this way. In many ways, what had been intended had made it possible for them to survive that winter. Without the *Mayflower* who knows what might have happened? The crew had been eager and willing workers and had played a terrific part in establishing this colony. A number of their own men had been lost through that winter so they had shared in both the despair and joy. Carver then decided, after some discussion with the rest of the elders, that it would be extremely unfair to let the Captain and his crew return to face the wrath of the financiers. A promissory note was written for Captain Jones to carry back to England. This explained both the reason for their predicament and their solemn intention to comply fully with the initial agreement, but requested that the time period should be extended.

It was a very sad day when the pilgrims stood along the shore of New Plymouth shouting and waving their goodbyes to the *Mayflower*. They had fondly embraced one another and said their farewells and there had been plenty of promises that some would return. The crew that now manned the ship was well short of the numbers that had brought it over but Captain Jones had assured the elders that he would make his journey to England. The anchor was hoisted and the *Mayflower* sailed slowly away towards the horizon on April 5th 1621 half loaded with goods and restocked for the survival of the journey. The pilgrims had lost good friends, so it took a while for them to come to terms with this and to begin seriously once more the task before them.

During that following year the pilgrims made good use of land, sea and forest as they began to master the habitat. They were always aware that they may well have to face a similar winter next time as the one that had just passed, bringing with it all of the hardships and threats to their survival that the previous one had. But this time they would be better prepared and they talked long and hard about it, identifying the things that they needed to do to ensure just this. The planting that had been done by both pilgrim, and Indian alike, began to bring its reward. Everything that they had brought with them for this purpose had been carefully sown and tended. But to add to this they had the benefits of what the Wampanoag had given to them. Although unable to recognise much of this seed it had been sewn and nurtured expectantly. They realised that their lives depended upon a good crop. It was therefore even more gratifying when they now started to pick new and wonderful crops from their land; some were crops that none had ever seen before in England and had no idea of their names or use. Fortunately for them, Squanto never once left their sides from the day he had first appeared in the distance spying upon the Winslows. He knew exactly what the crops were and what needed to be done with them to make them both edible and nourishing. They were particularly successful with a crop of what Squanto called 'maize', which they had never before seen. They also had wheat and peas in abundance.

The relationship between the Wampanoags and the pilgrims was very successful. Several of the Indian braves and squaws helped on the land and enough produce was grown to send food back to the Indian camp. In return the pilgrims received some wonderful produce back from the natives. Side by side they toiled the land and Squanto's relationship with the Winslows blossomed. His English improved greatly and he understood better each day what was said to him. The Winslows, who were experienced farmers, were able to teach the Wampanoag many of their ways of successful agriculture, but they also gained, in return, new knowledge from this partnership and the agricultural work was clearly well organised. Miles Standish had not needed to put any of his security plans into operation, so consequently he was left with the time to organise hunting and fishing expeditions. This brought great reward with small animals and fish in abundance. If the pilgrims discovered that they were ever in short supply of any commodity, then they would trade with their Indian partners. Knives and beads brought from England were exchanged for beaver skins and corn. Miles struck up a relationship with one Indian similar to that which the Winslows had made with Squanto. His name was 'Samoset'. He too had had previous contact with the English and he was an expert with the local fishing and hunting. He was able to show Miles and his group where to fish and the best Indian methods of trapping.

The friendship agreement made with the Wampanoags was one of the wisest decisions that the pilgrims could have made. It was obviously the pilgrims' religious practices and inoffensive attitudes towards their fellow man that gained them both the trust and the dedication that was shown to them by the Indians. Both groups lived in harmony and seemed just as important to one another. The pilgrims were no longer afraid of the local natives, this having been one of the prime concerns before their arrival. Over a period of time they developed complacency towards this, and took it for granted that all of the local inhabitants would be as friendly. Then one day an Indian previously unknown to every one arrived at the colony. He initially appeared to offer no offence and to have the same friendly disposition as all of the others, but he carried with him a snakeskin. Just as Squanto had done before, he had watched them closely in their agricultural toil before making his approach. He handed this snakeskin to the Winslows, who immediately believed it to be a very unusual gift. When they examined it more closely they found that there were several arrowheads embedded within it. They decided that they would deliver both this new native and the snakeskin to Miles Standish as they did not understand the meaning of it themselves. Miles interpreted this as bad news. Samoset had at one time told Miles of this kind of warning, explaining that if this was ever to occur then it must be taken as a threat. This Indian was obviously from a more distant tribe and was acting as a messenger. By delivering the snakeskin he hoped that the pilgrims might leave before risking conflict. Miles discussed this with the elders and Samoset and decided the course of action that they would follow. The snakeskin had its arrowheads removed and in their place were substituted with bullets. It was then given back to the messenger, who was sent away unharmed. The pilgrims renewed their vigil of the early days but fortunately for them they never saw or heard anything more of the messenger or his tribe.

After this occurrence it was decided that reinforcements should be made to the stockade. They constructed huge gates that would be fitted and closed every night after dusk fell. The children who had slowly become braver and who played daily outside the vicinity of the camp were now stopped from doing this for a while. A guard was constantly posted over the agricultural workers whilst they toiled. Ousamequin was consulted and he pledged his continuing loyalty to the treaty between them. Everyone now felt secure once more and Miles gradually released his grip upon security; over a period of time things returned back to normality.

Mary Brewster continued with the education of the children for several hours of the day ably assisted by Katherine Carver and Rose Standish, but now they also taught those children of the Wampanoag who wished to attend. Liza, and many of the oldest children, helped to maintain the hall and carry out general repairs. They did the sewing, made the clothes and did the cleaning. Oceanis thrived as the youngest of the colony's residents receiving a great deal of feminine attention that continued until the first of the New Plymouth babies were born; the first being the offspring of John Alden and Priscilla Mullins. All of John's hard work and the loyalty of Miles Standish had paid off eventually. This marriage had taken place in the first month of arrival and had been the first community ceremony in the new hall. William Brewster had conducted the service and at long last Rose Standish had been able to accept Miles's intentions as being completely honourable. Unfortunately for Rose and Miles the letters that she had placed in the possession of Captain Jones had long since left for England.

By the time the autumn of 1621 had finally arrived, and their first summer harvest gathered, the pilgrims were overwhelmed with the success that they had had in their first year. Along with the grown crops they also had quantities of water birds and wild turkeys. To everyone's delight the forest had been found to be full of deer and so venison was regularly eaten. A newly constructed stock house contained vast amounts of goods that would honour the debt they still owed to their investors. William Brewster, after consulting with the elders, was filled with the joy of this success and freedom, so he suggested that a thanksgiving day must be held. In this celebration they could offer praise to the Lord for the wealth and good fortune that he had bestowed upon them. The meeting hall was colourfully decorated with all manner of fruits and vegetables and the long tables were set out end to end. These tables with their bench seats had been constructed out of the wood taken from the gigantic pines that grew everywhere about them. It was a social gathering that would include everyone. This meant that the Wampanoag were invited too. Having long since been cleared of its original mass of tools and goods from home this hall could now be appreciated at its best. It was, indeed, a huge open space and a credit to those who had laboured upon it in such harsh conditions.

For this occasion all of the women and the eldest of the daughters had prepared a wonderful feast. Along the entire length of the tables were roasted wild turkeys, waterfowl, cobs of buttered corn and an abundance of vegetables. The Indian tribe had brought with them their contribution of both food and table decorations. John Carver sat at the top table, to his left sat William Brewster, and to his right sat Chief Ousamequin Massaoit. Today the Chief, not wishing to be over burdened with headdress, wore only a double spike of yellow and red feathers whilst the Puritans dressed in their most formal Sunday clothes with tall hats and ruffs. Each place setting had a small present wrapped and placed before it, finished off with delicate little bows. There were jugs of water and fruit cordials within easy reach of everyone. The ladies and the eldest children sat together in a group and the youngest children were seated separately and were as well supplied. Before anything was eaten a religious service was held where Grace was said and then everyone gave their thanks to their God. After the completion of the meal the tables and the general clutter were moved, so that the room was cleared. The floors had been scrubbed white that morning and were now brushed and made ready. The Brewster's old clavichord brought all the way from England was in position with Love Brewster seated before it. Some of the men had fiddles, mouth organs and whistles and several of the braves sat cross-legged upon the floor with drums tucked tightly between their thighs. There had been other informal music gatherings and music at the Sunday worship, but never before had the hall seen such a loud and lively occasion as this. Everyone danced including Ousamequin and the smallest of the children. This was a night of thanksgiving never to be forgotten.

This first year in the new homeland had been a very arduous test of character. It had begun with the loss of life of half of their lifelong friends and companions. They did not arrive to a warm greeting, instead they had their first little skirmish with the Indians, and then it had taken more time to discover the place they now inhabited. Many people may not have endured what they had been through in order to reach the position that they were now at and this was a credit to them. Being unable to fulfil their contracted promise had been especially hard upon a group of religious stalwarts who believed deeply in paying their debt and maintaining their honour. They had worked through the first four months in Plymouth in the most difficult of weather conditions, and all of this was achieved at a time when their own loved ones back on board the *Mayflower* were dying of the most horrible ailments.

God may have sent them the Wampanoag, for who is to say what may have become of them if they had confronted a less friendly tribe? They had been a source of constant local information and knowledge, and they too had sweated and grafted alongside their neighbours. At the worst of times the Puritans drew upon their immense depth of faith and this supported them at all times. They appreciated and supported each other as brothers and sisters in one large extended family. The strength of love between them and the love of their God provided a solid foundation rock on which to build.

So they entered into the New Year with pride, hope and faith. They had already begun to reap the rewards of their hard toil and the harvests had been plentiful enough to sustain them. Religious pressure was defunct; they worshipped as they saw fit, and they made, and lived by, their own rules and governed themselves. No King or Archbishop could now dictate to them and there was no constant watchful eye and threat of retribution. John Carver proved to be a wonderful choice of Governor. He governed by consent, discussing openly all options and no actions were ever taken without mutual agreement. William Brewster remained forever the father figure, uncle and Grandfather. He supported everyone. His door was never closed as he guided, blessed, encouraged and cried with them. William Bradford, everyone's right hand man, did exactly the same and he made things happen. Miles Standish remained a man of immense strength who they all trusted and worked closely with. The pilgrims relied upon his judgement and advice, and it was because of his presence that many slept soundly in their beds. It is probably wrong to select this quartet of leaders because all acted as one. Each gave strength and received it in turn, and all had a fair slice of wisdom. Every man, woman and child was enriched with the determination and courage to succeed.

* * *

Once more the wailing, harsh cutting winds, the continuing cruel cold and the smothering snow imprisoned them within their new homes. Only this time they had experience, and foresight and they had community. They also had warm beds, log fires and lacked for nothing to eat. So, as they entered the dark tunnel of winter, they stayed focussed upon the tiny glimmer of light that sparkled and beckoned calling them ever onward towards its distant end. They looked forward to it and what they might achieve next. It grew in luminance; it became candlelight, the rising dawn and then a drowning effervescence that saturated the entire habitat bursting forth into spring. During this time they had seen much less of the Wampanoag, but they had made it distinctively clear that this home was there for them too should conditions become unbearable. It had only been on the occasional forays of Miles Standish, and some of his companions, as they searched for fresh meat or fish that their paths had crossed. Other than this, unless the weather improved a little, no one ventured further than the gates of the stockade. With the stockpile of food available to them and their own livestock now being fruitful there was little reason to hunt, but the adventurous and the restless became hungry for action. Slowly the snows of that winter melted away and once more the sun began to warm both the soil and their hearts. Then suddenly, when everything looked brilliant and they thought that nothing more could happen to blight their lives, without prior warning on April 5th John Carver died.

Carver's death came as a terrific shock and was a tremendous hammer blow to everyone. From the highest pinnacle upon the mountain of life suddenly they were plunged into the darkest and deepest ravine of death. Until this time the community hall and church had been used only for joyous occasions, a place of worship, baptisms and celebration. Now it was being prepared for the first funeral and not just any funeral, but the funeral of a man whom they had all glorified. The first Governor of the new colony had been snatched from their midst after no more than twelve short months. Aged only forty-five with everything to live for; he was respected and held in high esteem by all. He had been expected to govern over them for many years to come. Imagine how Katherine felt. And imagine how every single member of his family in God felt at this time. Katherine was totally inconsolable. She had travelled to the distant corners of the earth to enjoy a new exciting life with her devoted husband, but now she had nothing. They were not blessed with children, although she had everyone else's children in a way. This is true, and she had their empathy.

Every funeral is solemn and this was truly a solemn affair. A graveyard, not thought about until now, had to be hurriedly designated and prepared. Carver's final resting place would need to be a place of honour and nobody would argue this point. A sloping piece of land to the rear of the stockade was agreed to be most suitable. It rose to a place with a craggy rock and a clump of trees. It had been deemed unsuitable for now to be used for agriculture, and it had always been a place where individuals in a solemn mood or families with picnics had climbed in order to satisfy their minds and bodies. It overlooked the stockade, the forest and the river winding its way in the distance and its vantage point revitalised souls.

Ousamequin attended the funeral, once again dressed in full regalia, along with four of the tribes elders, who were all dressed immaculately. So were their squaws and Squanto and Samoset were there to represent the tribe. It was a day to be written into the history books and never to be forgotten. Stephen had the honour of carving the headstone from a chunk of rock taken from the summit. It was an ordeal to have to carry out but he did it conscientiously; it was a real labour of love to have to do such a thing for one so close. It read:

R.I.P.
John Carver
1576-1621
Loving husband to Katherine
First Governor of
New Plymouth Colony.

Since the early days of death aboard the *Mayflower*, and the suffering they had endured since to reach this moment, this was to be their darkest day. They needed God more on this day to lift them up and to renew their vision more than any day before.

Of course, the death left them without a political leader. Some immediately looked to Brewster, who by now had become really well established in his role as church Pastor, and it was fair to say, that he was happy with his lot. Others spoke of the strength of character and leadership of Standish. They recognised the valuable contribution that he had made towards establishing them there. Ever since the day he had been introduced to some in Leiden he had appeared to act tirelessly in their interests. But surprisingly enough, the quiet, organised and unflappable William Bradford emerged as the majority choice. He had always been a stalwart supporter of Brewster. For a long period known in Scrooby and even after his own personal loss of

Dorothy May, coming before she had even had chance to set foot upon this new land, leaving him without a partner, never did he let this personal grief waiver his intent.

William Bradford was shocked, amused and immensely proud that he might even be suggested in this capacity. He was thirty years of age, younger than some, and he believed there were much better men than he, but they did not. When it came to the decision William Bradford was elected unanimously, just as his predecessor before him had been. He was both humbled by the support he had received and bemused, however he accepted and was duly sworn in, pledging his life to serving the pilgrims, as the Second Governor of New Plymouth.

To lose John Carver so suddenly and at such a time was a real blow to the pilgrims. He was Brewster's closest ally and one of the true driving forces behind the new colony. It's true to say that he was not the initiator of the move, but he had been one of its greatest activists and motivators. Carver loved the people of Scrooby so much that he and his wife Katherine had left the higher strata of society life in London, England in order to be where they were today. He had been a good loyal friend and companion to all who knew him. He had used his contacts and good offices in order that he might appropriate opportunities and funding for the Puritans. Carver was not the most practical of persons. He was not the one to handle heavy loads, or to bear the physical ability of the digging of foundations, but he had a way of getting these things done. With his ingenuity and excellent common sense he had been able to metamorphosise the chrysalis into the butterfly.

Chapter Eleven

The First Ten Years

Bradford knew that he could never replace John Carver, but he too had worked many hours in order to raise columns upon padstones. Since the early days, when he had helped with the process of collecting names and planning, he had spent the greatest part of his life with his villagers around him. He had developed into a public official. He knew and loved his people. He too shared their desires and their heartaches. He pledged from this day forward that his entire existence would be spent in devotion toward the Puritan cause. Since losing Dorothy May, he had carried an unbearable guilt in his heart, even though his friends had repeatedly assured him that he could have done nothing more. He had felt lonely without her and had it not been for the companionship that he had received within the group he could well have given up on life too. The love that he had left to give now would be taken over by his enthusiasm for the success of the colony.

The winter that had just passed had been much less harsh than its predecessor. The achievements that had been made in that first full year had been exceptional for such a small group. All those who had wanted them now had their own individual homes. There were several public facilities either completed, under construction, or planned. The first summer harvest had been good and they had met the natives and learned to live amicably alongside them. It had always been the plan that at the right time, hopefully not too far into the future, that they would be joined by others of their beliefs. Some had left their families in Leiden because the list that had been composed there meant that there had been far too many to travel with them. Perhaps now some of these people still wanted to come. There were even people back home in England whom some wished might hear of their achievements and still come to them now. Liza still daydreamed that at sometime in the future she might throw her arms once again around Harriet and her daughter, Natalie.

There had been no contact with the outside world for a long period now. Since the *Mayflower* had sailed off into the distance it had been just the pilgrims and the Wampanoag. They knew nothing of the state of the world and it was presumed that the world knew little of them. Had their folk back in England or Leiden ever received the messages that they had sent back with Captain Jones? In fact, had the half-manned *Mayflower* ever been able to successfully return? All could have been presumed lost at sea and they would have been none the wiser. If it hadn't been for the fact that they were so committed and determined any of these thoughts might have depressed the strongest of souls.

The first year's successes continued through into the present one. The cooperation between the races grew and they faced no new threats. The first year's agricultural experiences expanded. The Winslows and their helpers understood their crops. A supply chain of food was established as they started to know exactly what they needed when. They began to stagger and rotate their crops. They used every bit of local knowledge that was passed on to them and they shared their own with their native partners. There were still new surprises that came along including more wonderful local crops being introduced to them for the first time. There was one that they had no name for. It had yellow flowers on at first, followed by green berries that grew into a small red fruit. These grew in bunches on green ground plants a few feet high. They contained small pips and tasted slightly sour, but they were refreshing and completely edible. The forests and waterways held food in abundance and now that the majority of the building works were completed there was more time to adventure out further. Life in the stockade became more relaxed, with the birth of Alden and Priscilla's baby imminent, everyone looked forward to another huge social event at the christening.

Stephen, Liza and the four children were all thriving. They had more of everything here and seldom now did they discuss Scrooby. Occasionally it was slipped into the conversation with a flashback of recollected memory, but neither had ever said, 'we wish we were back home'. They were the parents of four beautiful, well-educated children. Education had been of supreme importance to the Puritans from the offset. They believed that people with small minds and even smaller ambitions had been responsible for the English attitude towards their faith. They were also extremely fortunate to have such wonderful role models around daily for the children. It hadn't only been Mary Brewster and Katherine Carver's teaching; it had also had much to do with the influence of John Carver, William Brewster, Bradford, Miles Standish and the Winslows.

As everyone became settled and looked more to the future they started to rekindle their own personal desires. Stephen began to re-establish himself around horses which had always been his passion. His opportunity arose on the day when Squanto rode in on a horse that appeared to have a slight limp which he examined, finding that it had a small growth upon the hoof and he was able to correct it. Over the next few weeks other horses were brought to him to look at and then he was given a horse by Ousamequin. The pilgrims had not taken any horses with them, so this was the first horse to be owned by one of them. Needless to say Stephen was a very proud man. Following this event he went out with Squanto and Samoset to gather in some of the wild horses that roamed the plains. He made himself a little fenced area and stable and installed a hearth to work upon the horse tackle. His old blacksmith days yearned to be released from within him having lain dormant since before their move to Leiden. Liza supported him in his desires, as did the children. Liza kept herself busy working for the community.

Ely had, once his part had been played in the construction works, tried to re-establish himself upon the water. He began modestly by carving out canoes from some of the timbers, but with great support from others, particularly William Trevore. They soon began to build more seaworthy boats. A jetty was constructed stretching out from the beach into the sea, which allowed them to tie off the boats and canoes and take them away from the shallow waters. It was also a great favourite in the summer months for the swimmers amongst them. Most of the older children loved it, so the pilgrims held gatherings there till late into the evening on the finest days. So soon a larger and much grander one was constructed. There was no shortage of good timber and they saw no reason not to be preparing for the future. The one limitation that they faced now was in the shortage of good sailcloth or the materials to make it. Ely, much to his credit and foresight, had done excellently indeed to obtain from Captain Jones, before they left, the remains of the *Mayflower's* sail that had been damaged in the storm. From this they had made the sails for a reasonable sized sailboat, which allowed them to venture further off the coast. He couldn't wait for a supply of cloth to be brought in; expressing this to William Brewster, knowing that this had been added to the list sent back with the *Mayflower*.

Ely, who was usually present upon the shoreline, was there to witness first-hand his wish come true as he sat upon the 'grand jetty' with his legs dangling, busily carving out a new oar. He was the one who screeched most loudly, at the top of his voice, and danced a merry jig upon the boards, when he spotted the approaching masts of a ship far out to sea but definitely coming their way. His shouting attracted much attention, but mainly from the children, so he despatched one of them hurriedly to find William Bradford, Brewster and Standish. At first Miles, forever their protector, had concerns that the approaching ship might not be friendly and that it may well be a pirate ship. It was November 11th 1621 and as they stood looking out towards the ocean a mass of pilgrims gathered around. Brewster stood there examining the ship through a long telescope whilst Bradford sent off some of the men to bring arms back to the shore as a precaution.

The precautions that were taken proved to be totally unnecessary when Brewster declared that he had spotted the English flag being flown. The vessel approached slowly inward causing everyone to grow anxious, until eventually, it stood still and they witnessed the anchor being slid away. To some the picture of the *Mayflower* swam through their minds just as it had been, sitting there in the bay for that long period of time. This ship could not have been moored above twenty or thirty feet differently in any direction. The pilgrims believed that they could hear loud singing and cheering in the distance and they were not wrong. Now they saw arms and anything within reach on board being waved at them from the decks. It took just a short time for a launch to be dropped and when he saw this it shook

Ely back to his senses. He quickly beckoned some of the others to follow him and to take some of the small boats out to greet them. None of the colony knew just who might be here calling upon them, but Brewster knew it was not the *Mayflower* returned. Uncannily, some of them started to behave completely out of character, call it a sixth sense, but as the launch approached the jetty, the Winslow brothers pushed people aside, in their haste, as they ran anxiously towards it. The first man to step out of the launch reacted likewise and sprinted at them casting his baggage aside. The others watched in amazement as all three threw their arms about each other and jigged a circle out onto the sands. Others left the launch and headed towards some of the otherwise restrained but bemused onlookers. They later discovered that the first man ashore had been John Winslow.

John and the two other Winslow brothers had vowed to stay on in England and his arrival had prompted Edward and Gilbert to believe that all the Winslow brothers had arrived that day. Kenhelm and Josiah were not there, but they were still pleased that one of their long lost brothers had returned to be with them. They took some tearing apart, but as some of the other Scrooby folk realised who it was they too took their turn in welcoming John. He was bombarded with questions from people longing to hear about other Scrooby neighbours. The ship that had arrived was the *Fortune* and it carried in total another thirty-five settlers to this new colony of Plymouth. John Winslow explained to everyone how he had travelled south and lodged there for three months in order that he might take any ship that was heading out from there. News had arrived at his lodgings early one morning that a ship laden with refugees from Holland had sailed into port intent upon travelling to the New World to join their families. John had paid his way along with all of the others, a few more being old Scrooby friends, and he boarded the *Fortune* for Plymouth, America.

Unfortunately, the new settlers carried with them a letter of complaint from the *Mayflower's* sponsors, those who had financially supported the first emigration, but had not had their contract honoured. Where was their promised cargo? The initial load that had reached them fell far below either expectation or valuation. The pilgrims, never having any ill intent, had always been determined that they must pay their debt. Sufficient goods had been stockpiled in order to honour this commitment and Brewster assured the *Fortune's* first mate that when they left they would leave full to the brim. William Brewster was determined to make good both the reputation and character of the pilgrims, and to this effect he swiftly penned a letter to be returned to England. He had all the elders append their signatures and William Bradford signed in his capacity as the new governor of Plymouth, America.

This note was taken back to the Captain who had remained on board his ship with another simple note that read: 'We invite the Captain and his full crew to join us ashore tomorrow evening for a reception in the Plymouth Community hall where you will be made most welcome, fed and entertained'. Imagine the gaiety that followed with their loved ones appearing unexpectedly and also knowing that a special party was now being arranged for everyone upon the following day. There was much catching up to do, as well as places to be found for the newcomers to sleep. Their reception to this land would be far more comfortable than the one that the first pilgrims had received before them. So that following evening, Ely sailed across to inform the Captain that they were expected. He escorted some ashore and the 'new comers', as they now became known, joined the 'old comers' along with the *Fortune's* full complement of crew, barring one watchman. A lavish feast was laid out and a dance held just as it was whenever the community had something special to celebrate, and this was extra special.

Over the next week the launch and several of the community's small boats went to and fro between the *Fortune* and land delivering to it a stockpile of goods until it was agreed that the ship could not hold any more. During this time, most of the elders went out to the ship and spent time on board as the Captain's guests. Besides the very lengthy letter, that he had penned, Brewster was also adamant that the Captain should also convey his own verbal expression of the gratitude they felt, and hoped now that these goods would suffice. He made it clear that if it had not been for the severity of their position upon arrival such delays would not have occurred. The Captain also agreed to return home with various letters of communication, some of which were addressed to Sir Edwin Sandys. Brewster having realised that he could not express his debt of gratitude in any greater detail than he had, and knowing that the *Fortune* was now entirely loaded prominently with lumber and beaver furs, believed that the Puritans had honoured the contract and that the ship should make haste.

So the *Fortune* was with them only for the shortest of periods and then it left for England. It left behind it a colony almost doubled that in size than before it arrived. Besides the new pilgrims that had arrived, it had also brought along valuable commodities that were very useful for their continuing survival and future development. The *Fortune* made good speed leaving behind the pilgrims who were now elated in the knowledge that they were now in no one's debt. However, unknowingly to the people of New Plymouth, the *Fortune* proved to be very 'unfortunate', because it was challenged upon the high seas by a French man-o-war and was sunk along with its cargo. It would be another year before the pilgrims were made aware of this fact.

In England the financiers were extremely angry with the pilgrims' lack of respect for their plight and were still without recompense or explanation.

With a trio of Winslows now reunited and other family members with wives and children returned to them, work in and around the colony gained in momentum. Extra hands helped to take on the workload and construction recommenced. This meant that a side of the stockade was removed and, because of the general feeling of security, the timber was used in a more resourceful way. Even now the Indian braves sometimes brought rumours of unfriendly tribes, but the pilgrims still did not experience any of this. John Winslow explained to his brothers how both of the two remaining brothers and their families had had intentions at some time in the future to join them. Of course Edward and Gilbert were overjoyed with this news, realising that they must plan for the future possibility of the complete family reunion. John's arrival had been a powerful surprise, but if the remaining members of the family were to arrive, then this would fulfil their wildest ambitions.

Part of this newfound Winslow spirit and ambition was responsible for them developing a much larger and grander homestead attached to the farmlands. This was achieved with the full blessing of the elders. So along with the farming toil of the day they worked late into the nights, chopping, dragging and fixing timbers. They had more than enough willing helpers. It kept them engrossed, but Edward, who was carried away by it all, failed to notice that Gilbert had become more withdrawn since his brothers' arrival. He laboured just as hard as the other two, but instead of futuristic dreams he constantly enquired of England, Scrooby and the farm. He was unusually quiet compared to the man he had been. It took a long period before Edward recognised this in Gilbert and asked what was troubling him. All of the talk of England had awakened a sleeping torment and he pined for England, the land of his birth. Edward understood this but he reminded Gilbert that just as John had come to them then there soon would be no reason why they could not return to visit England. The *Fortune*, he said, would be the first of many to follow. For the moment this appeared to be sufficient to lift Gilbert, and Edward these days, always the master of the right expression, was sincere in his suggestion.

Every subsequent winter seemed easier than the first allowing the pilgrims some progress even upon the dowdiest of days. But the newcomers had only the stories from the old comers of how big, bountiful and beautiful this new land truly was. Edward Winslow set up a meeting in which the newcomers might all be introduced formally to Chief Ousamequin Massaoit, which he believed to be the right and proper thing to do. He wanted to introduce them all and to show to the Indians that these people were their people too. He also wanted them all to acknowledge that they too respected the treaty that stood between them. He had Bradford's support in this as the Governor appreciated Edward's good intentions, also recognising the diplomatic ability that he possessed. The Winslows had been the first to make contact with their neighbours and had throughout the relationship shown a great deal of goodwill and respect towards them. Bradford, considering the increased size of the colony and recognising the strengths in others, considered his position as the Governor and he discussed this with Brewster. It is reasonable to say that he saw Bradford for what he was and recognised that the power invested in him was worthy of the man, but Bradford insisted that every year a new election should be held in order to give others the right to vote. This went ahead merely in order to appease him and he took the Governorship once more without any opposition.

Throughout the year of 1622 Gilbert Winslow never ceased in reminding his brother that he still desired to see England and should the first opportunity arrive then he would want to take it. The opportunity, as he put it, was out of all of their control; they awaited the next arrival of a large ship to their shores and what that may bring to them. Edward realised that Gilbert's desire was becoming obsessive, and having never previously discussed it with the elders, he decided that he should.

Brewster and Bradford were as shocked as Edward had originally been, but after further discussions with Edward, they began to see it as he encouraged them to. He thought it a positive step that someone might travel between the colony and England representing and arguing their case and arranging trade. So it was agreed that Gilbert should have the blessing of the others, and if he was in agreement then he could represent them all back in England. From then on, they began to plan for ways that he should help and produced lists of items that they had a need for but could not obtain. The colony constantly stockpiled goods knowing that they might one day become trade-offs and Gilbert would have the advantage of these. John, who had settled in really well, was also a little dismayed that his brother should want to return but he too, like Edward, was eventually convinced through Gilbert's sincere commitment to such a journey.

The newcomers soon realised that after all of the time spent in the wilderness, this new colony allowed them all of the freedom that they might ever have prayed for. As new American Protestants they set their own agenda; there were no longer any restrictive practices. They were able to discuss freely and openly at any time of night or day their religious beliefs, independent of all external influence and unanswerable to nobody. They now lived in the belief that they owed no external debt and owed only unto God. They were a family in communion, each together, brothers and sisters alike. With the Wampanoag they had their friendship, trust and treaty but each had independence from the other. They expected what they had built to increase in size, this they were prepared for, and unless anything unforeseen came along then the population would swell. They just had to wait now for a new ship upon the horizon; in due time it arrived.

In 1623, the *'Anne and Little James'* sailed graciously into the cove and brought along with it the now accustomed celebration. It brought more settlers and more valuable commodities to this new land. Edward Winslow needed no new prompting by Gilbert, who hastily made ready for departure. He was aware of his commitment to the community there and one such commitment was, that he should carry with him the simplest of messages to be delivered to any still in persecution, 'there was a land where they would be welcomed and persecution did no longer exist'. He would also negotiate on behalf of the community the best of deals that he could find in exchange for the stockpile of goods that were to be transported to England with him.

The setback now was that this new ship's Captain was also the bearer of bad tidings. He informed them of the previous loss to pirates of the *'Fortune'*. This meant that there were new concerns for the elders and they wondered if Gilbert's life would be safe considering the *Fortune's* demise. Gilbert was not to be deterred and he fully intended to take any risk to return this time to England. Edward would not accept this and much debate and argument followed before a final decision ensued. Edward insisted that he accompany Gilbert. John, having arrived last, was to continue representing them in their absence. They, for their part, promised that if sufficient enough goods could be packed into this ship then they had no fear of accompanying it and delivering the payload. They would also try to ensure that, if there were still sufficient goods, then they would be used wisely and thriftily, enough to bargain for some of the community's more vital needs. The elders saw that the Winslows were determined to see this through, deciding they would not stand in their way and neither would John. The Winslows would carry back with them messages and then stay long enough to do everything that was intended. This included spending time with the Winslows in Scrooby before finding the first passage back to America.

The Anne and Little James stayed just long enough to experience the New Plymouth's hospitality and to reload. When it made sail outward bound it carried aboard the first New World diplomats. It left behind a loving brother who had not expected to be in this position at all, waving them out of sight before returning to the fields as the new Winslow principal. Edward, for one, was determined to make a success of this because it meant so much to the colony to see these debts settled. He had other important issues to pursue of which he had discussed in detail with the elders. John, it seemed, had been the most sacrificial of the brothers, having reunited himself with them after all that time, he now found that he was the only Winslow in New Plymouth and that he carried their responsibilities in their leave. He was very proud of his brothers, especially the achievements that they had made here, and the attitude that they both displayed towards representing their community. In his short time there he had already realised just how differently people's esteem had risen from the Scrooby days and of how highly his family name was held. In their absence he was resolved in not letting them down.

He held the responsibility for less than twelve months. The frequency of ships to this their new homeland was growing ever faster. News that had reached England and Holland obviously carried the success of the colony. Edward arrived home triumphantly. John greeted him with the broadest of smiles and the usual jig. He quickly looked around at the other passengers who milled about them, but he could not make out another familiar face. One major hope had been that with this visit other members of their family might have been encouraged enough by the brother's message to have joined them upon the return voyage. But where was Gilbert? Not only could he not see other members of his family, he did not see Gilbert. When Edward explained that Gilbert would not return as swiftly as he had, he went on to add that he had his doubts that Gilbert would ever return at all. This was devastating news for John and, of course, everyone else that soon became aware of this.

They had, however, achieved all of their aims. Debts were honoured, apologies accepted and their good name reinstated. There were more than enough goods to do as they had wished. Communications had been passed on and they brought back more by return. Edward had even spent time in London with Sir Edwin Sandys, who it appeared had been fighting for their good name with those who were owed debts back in England knowing William Brewster to be a man of honour. Edward believed that his only failure had been a personal one. He knew how much John wished for the Winslows to be reunited and not further distanced. He too had that same wish but this time it had not worked out. He had been happy to be reunited with the others and he had suffered his own twinge of homesickness, but he too was a man of honour and intended to do right by the community. As for the family, well, he could tell John he honestly felt that at some time in the future some, if not all of them, would be reunited together in America.

The elders arranged a formal meeting with him so that all could gauge the response of the old homeland towards their little group. They all wanted to hear of the details of how the trading progressed, and just how much they could expect to achieve. With this he could give them the most encouraging news of companies who had approached him asking to trade with them; Sir Edwin Sandys also had taken it upon himself to make legal any business that occurred using his own good offices for that purpose. One huge surprise was still in store for them, he said – presently being unloaded from the ship were what both he and Gilbert had most hoped to bring back with them, twenty English milking cows and a bull, all having survived the journey. This brought loud whoops of cheer and hats were thrown up into the air. They hoped that these were to be the first of many and that they could start to breed them upon American soil. Of course, this ensured that another great celebration was held with the entire ship's crew invited too.

Throughout the first ten years the community expanded vastly. The friendship forged between them and the ever-growing Wampanoag tribe continued in strength, living side by side and sharing in their expanding society. The small group of cottages around the main hall had developed into a village. Everyone knew and respected their neighbours and all kept faith in God and each shared in each other's success. Ships continued to frequent the New Plymouth port taking goods away and making deliveries to them and forever bringing new people to these shores. Edward Winslow, having been so successful in his first diplomatic role, followed on with many more trips abroad whenever he was requested to do so. For many years he was a vital lifeline between the New World and the Old; he was their most trusted representative. He never went to England without visiting Scrooby and he always tried to encourage his family to return with him. His message to John was always the same that one day he believed that Kenhelm and Josiah would accompany him back. He knew now that Gilbert had had his taste of America and that he had vowed to be content to die in England.

In 1629 the second *'Mayflower'* reached the shores of New Plymouth. This ship, a rebuild of the original *Mayflower*, made its journey fully in the knowledge of the impact that it would have upon the people there. They had not underestimated this. As it approached to drop anchor Ely had already got messages back to the elders, and the beach and jetties were awash with bodies. All cheered loudly, and instruments were played and singing commenced. Some even cried as they remembered those days of hardship with the loss of so many loved ones. It brought with it even greater trade and more settlers. Then it stayed on for longer than its time to become involved in the carnival atmosphere that it alone had created. In 1630 seventeen ships, anchored off New Plymouth having travelled in a fleet, all carried Puritans to this New World and new life, reuniting once again families and friends so long separated.

William Bradford was re-elected time and time again and William and Mary Brewster continued on as father and mother to an ever-expanding family. Miles Standish was still their protectorate, and all of those who had since joined John Carver, long since gone, within the graveyard, overlooked a population that grew and grew. Stephen and Liza Hopkins were now Grandpa and Grandma Hopkins. Oceanis had now reached his tenth year. And none of this bore any resemblance whatsoever to that small village of Scrooby still lying unchanged within the leafy valleys of Nottinghamshire. These lives had changed dramatically forever. Every year, without fail, so that their success and achievement should be commemorated, a feast of thanksgiving is held in order to celebrate this and called, naturally, 'Thanksgiving Day'.

The will, the faith, the courage and the pride of the original group of Scrooby pilgrims had given birth to a whole new exciting World.

All who have great faith in God
Present your lives to him
Set sail upon the Ocean tide
To be a Pilgrim.

Bibliography

The English Renaissance   Edited by Kate Aughterson.
Encyclopedia of British History Philip Steele.
English Social History 1603 To Modern Times. L.W.Cowie.
The Junior World Encyclopaedia   Sampson Low London.

Websites
http://pilgrims.net/native_americans/massasoiy.html
http://pilgrims.net/plymouth/history/passengers.htm
http://pilgrims.net/Plymouth/history/
http://www.pilgrimarchives.nl/html/pilgrims/top_html/history.html
http://www.palouse.net/hobbies/shipstamps/topics/html/pilgrim.htm
http://en.wikipedia.org/wiki/Mayflower_compact
http://www.mike-reed.com/Travel%20Journal/Holland-Pilgrims.htm
http://wwwpilgrimfathers.visitnottingham.com/exec/
http://www.pilgrimhall.org/LeidenInfo.htm